# *Captain Corelli's Mandolin*

## LOUIS DE BERNIÈRES

Level 6

Retold by Mary Tomalin
Series Editors: Andy Hopkins and Jocelyn Potter

**Pearson Education Limited**
Edinburgh Gate, Harlow,
Essex CM20 2JE, England
and Associated Companies throughout the world.

ISBN 0 582 46135 9

First published in Great Britain by Martin Secker & Warburg Limited, London, 1994
This edition first published 2001

Typeset by Ferdinand Pageworks, London
Set in 11/14pt Bembo
Printed in Spain by Mateu Cromo, S. A. Pinto (Madrid)

Published by Pearson Education Limited in association with
Penguin Books Ltd, both companies being subsidiaries of Pearson Plc

For a complete list of the titles available in the Penguin Readers series please write to your local
Pearson Education office or to: Marketing Department, Penguin Longman Publishing,
5 Bentinck Street, London W1M 5RN.

# *Contents*

|  |  | page |
| --- | --- | --- |
| Introduction | | v |
| Chapter 1 | August 1940: The Doctor and his Daughter | 1 |
| Chapter 2 | Pelagia and Mandras | 8 |
| Chapter 3 | The Homosexual | 13 |
| Chapter 4 | The Wild Man | 18 |
| Chapter 5 | 30 April 1941: Invasion | 23 |
| Chapter 6 | The Freedom Fighter | 31 |
| Chapter 7 | A Problem with Eyes | 35 |
| Chapter 8 | Snails | 39 |
| Chapter 9 | Autumn 1943: Betrayal | 48 |
| Chapter 10 | The Order to Kill | 55 |
| Chapter 11 | An Operation | 60 |
| Chapter 12 | 1943-9: The Years of Terror | 69 |
| Chapter 13 | Antonia | 77 |
| Chapter 14 | 1953: Earthquake | 81 |
| Chapter 15 | Alexi | 87 |
| Chapter 16 | An Unexpected Lesson | 91 |
| Chapter 17 | The Return | 96 |
| Activities | | 102 |

# Publishers of *Captain Corelli's Mandolin*
## by Louis de Bernières

**English language**
**UK market**
Vintage Books, Random House Group

**US market**
Vintage Books, Random House Inc.

**Translations**

| | |
|---|---|
| **Brazil** | Distribuidora |
| **Czech Republic** | BB/art |
| **Denmark** | Rosinante/Munksgaard |
| **Estonia** | Varrak |
| **Finland** | Otava Publishing Co |
| **France** | Editions Denoel |
| **Germany** | Hoffmann & Campe (hardcover); |
| | S. Fischer Verlag (paperback) |
| **Greece** | Psichogios Publications |
| **Holland** | Uitgeverij Arbeiderspers |
| **Hungary** | Helikon Publishers |
| **Israel** | Zmora-Bitan |
| **Italy** | Longanesi (hardcover); TEA (paperback) |
| **Japan** | Tokyo Sogen |
| **Norway** | Pax Forlag |
| **Poland** | Proszynski i S-ka |
| **Portugal** | ASA Editores |
| **Slovakia** | Slovart |
| **Spain** | Plaza y Janes Ediciones |
| **Sweden** | Wahlstrom & Widstrand |
| **Turkey** | Yapi Kredi Kultur |

# Introduction

*It was hard for Pelagia to love an invader and sometimes she shouted at Corelli, her eyes filled with tears of anger: 'How can you bear to be here? Orders? Orders from a madman! Don't you know you're being used? Why don't you take your guns and leave? Don't you know who the enemy is?'*

*At these times the captain listened silently and bowed his head, the bitterness of his shame eating like a worm at the muscles of his heart. But they could not stop themselves from loving one another.*

The year is 1941. It is the time of the Second World War, and in Europe millions are dying. Germany and Italy have invaded Greece, and Italian troops have occupied the small Greek island of Cephallonia. An Italian officer, Captain Antonio Corelli, is given accommodation at the house of Dr Iannis and his pretty daughter Pelagia. They try hard to hate him, but the charming Corelli is an excellent musician and his mandolin-playing makes them forget that he is an invader. Soon Pelagia, who is engaged to a handsome young islander, finds that she has a problem . . .

*Captain Corelli's Mandolin* is a great love story, but it is also a powerful description of the tragedy and cruelty of war. History and fiction are combined in a way that makes this novel – and the island of Cephallonia – unforgettable.

Louis de Bernières was born in 1954 and has worked as a teacher, mechanic and gardener. In the early 1990s he published three novels set in South America. De Bernières won prizes for two of these novels but he is best known for *Captain Corelli's Mandolin*, published in 1994. The book received excellent reviews but little publicity; it became a bestseller as people read it and recommended it to their friends.

# Chapter 1    August 1940:
# The Doctor and his Daughter

Dr Iannis had enjoyed a satisfactory day in which none of his patients had died or got any worse. He had removed a tooth, attended the surprisingly easy birth of a lamb, and had performed a successful, though minor, operation.

He had been called to the house of old man Stamatis, who was suffering from earache. After gazing into the dark, hairy hole of the old man's ear, the doctor had cleaned up the inside of the ear using a matchstick, cotton wool and alcohol. He was aware that old man Stamatis had been deaf in that ear since childhood, but was nevertheless surprised when the tip of the matchstick touched something hard, something that had no excuse for its presence there. He took the old man to the window, where the light was better, and stared down into the ear again; then with his long matchstick he pushed the grey hairs to one side. There was something round inside. He scratched its surface and saw a pea. It was undoubtedly a pea; it was light green and slightly lined. Dr Iannis considered the problem for some moments, then requested a small fishhook and a light hammer.

The old man and his wife looked at each other with the single thought that the doctor must have lost his mind. 'What does this have to do with my earache?' asked Stamatis suspiciously. But the hook and hammer were fetched, and the doctor carefully placed the straightened hook into the hairy hole and raised the hammer. There was a terrible scream.

'Oh, oh, the fishhook will enter his brain. May God protect us!' cried the old wife, hiding her head in her hands.

This speech caused the doctor to pause and consider the possibility that the hammer might only drive the pea further into the ear. 'Change of plan,' he announced, and gave instructions that Stamatis should lie on his side till evening with his ear filled with warm water. He returned at six o'clock, hooked the softened pea successfully without the aid of a hammer, small or otherwise, and pulled it out. Stamatis clapped his hand to his ear and exclaimed, 'It's cold in there. My God, it's loud. I mean everything is loud!'

'Your deafness is cured,' announced Dr Iannis. 'A very satisfactory operation, I think.' Shortly afterwards he walked home with a fat chicken under each arm, and an ancient pea wrapped up in his handkerchief.

The doctor was now left with an entire evening in which to write his 'New History of Cephallonia', a project which he had begun at least a dozen times. He seemed unable to achieve objectivity and so had never been satisfied with the result. He sat down and wrote:

'The ancient, half-forgotten island of Cephallonia rises from the Ionian Sea,★ its rocks and red earth heavy with the heat of the sun and the weight of memory. In the stories of ancient Greece, the island played its part and had its gods – among them Poseidon, the god of the Sea and Apollo, the god of the Sun. Yes, once this island, with its brilliant light, its transparent waters, was an island filled with gods. But today Cephallonia has become a factory that breeds babies for export. There are more Cephallonians abroad or at sea than there are at home. There is no industry here that keeps families together, there is not enough agricultural land, there are not enough fish in the ocean. Our men go abroad and return here to die. The only good thing about it is that only the beautiful women find husbands among the men who are left, and consequently we have the most beautiful women in all of Greece . . .'

★ Ionian Sea: part of the Mediterranean Sea, between the southern part of Italy and Greece.

The doctor refilled his pipe and read this through. He listened to Pelagia moving about in the kitchen, preparing the evening meal. He read what he had written about beautiful women and remembered his wife, who had died from lung disease despite all his efforts and who had been as lovely as his daughter was now. 'This island betrays its own people,' he wrote, then seized the sheet of paper and threw it forcefully into the corner of the room. This was not good enough. Why could he not write like a writer of histories? Why could he not write without passion, without anger at the many betrayals and oppressions that the island had suffered in the past? He went outside for a breath of fresh air, returning indoors just in time to catch Pelagia's little goat eating his writings with a look of satisfaction on its face. He tore the paper from the animal's mouth, chased it outside, then marched into the kitchen. 'That unpleasant animal of yours has eaten everything I've written tonight,' he exclaimed crossly. 'Any more incidents like this, and it'll end up on our plates.'

Pelagia looked up at her father and smiled. 'We'll be eating at about ten o'clock.'

'Did you hear what I said? No more goats inside the house.'

Pelagia paused in her slicing of a tomato, brushed her hair from her face and replied, 'You're as fond of him as I am.'

Dr Iannis turned away, defeated. It was an annoying thing when a daughter spoke cheekily to him and reminded him of her mother at the same time. He returned to his table, took the title page, 'A New History of Cephallonia', and crossed out the first two words, writing instead, 'A Personal'. Now he could express his opinions as freely and unpleasantly as he wished.

♦

When Pelagia heard from a neighbour that a strongman was giving a performance in the village square, she put away her broom and hurried to join the group of curious islanders that had gathered there. Megalo Velisarios, famous all over the islands of Ionia as one of the strongest men who had ever lived, was jumping up and down in time to the clapping of hands. On each of his outstretched arms sat a full-grown man. One of them held on tightly to his body while the other calmly smoked a cigarette. On Velisarios's head sat an anxious little girl of about six years, who was making matters more complicated by holding her hands firmly across his eyes.

'Lemoni!' he roared. 'Take your hands from my eyes and hold on to my hair, or I'll have to stop.'

Lemoni was too frightened to move her hands and Megalo Velisarios stopped. With one graceful movement he threw both men to their feet, lifted Lemoni from his head, threw her high into the air and caught her, kissed her dramatically upon the tip of her nose and set her down. Raising himself to his full height, he cried, 'I will lift anything that it takes three men to lift.'

The village priest, Father Arsenios, chose just this moment to walk with a self-important expression across the square on his way to the church. He lacked respect, not because he was completely round but because he was greedy for both money and food and was much too interested in women.

'Lift Father Arsenios,' someone called.

'Impossible,' called another.

Father Arsenios quite suddenly found himself grasped around his chest and lifted up on to the wall. He sat there speechless with surprise, his mouth opening and closing like a fish, and a guilty silence descended. Pelagia felt her heart overflow with pity for the poor man. She stepped forward and extended a hand to help him down, and the priest walked off without a word. Pelagia now spoke sharply to Velisarios. She was only seventeen but she was proud and knew her own mind, and her position as the doctor's daughter meant that even the men were forced to respect her. 'You shouldn't have done that, Velisarios,' she said. 'It was cruel and horrible. You must apologize.'

He looked down at her from his great height. This was without doubt a difficult situation. He thought of lifting her above his head.

'We want to see the cannon,' called an old lady, and others in the crowd echoed her.

Velisarios was immensely proud of his ability to raise the old Turkish cannon, which had the date 1739 on it and was much too heavy for anyone else to lift. He looked down at Pelagia and said, 'I'll apologize later, pretty one,' then announced, 'Good people of the village, to see the cannon, you must bring me your old nails, your broken pots, and the stones of the streets. Find me these things while I pack the gun with powder.'

People ran off eagerly in all directions to seek out these objects, and the cannon was soon prepared for the great explosion. 'I will fire the gun down the road,' said Velisarios when all was made ready. 'Everybody out of the way now.'

With a theatrical expression, the enormous man put a match to the cannon and lifted it to his waist. Silence fell. Breaths were held. There was a great roar as the old pots and nails burst from the gun . . . and then a long, low cry of pain. There was a moment of confusion and hesitation. People looked around at each other to see who had been hit, and Velisarios dropped his cannon and ran forward to a young man lying in the dust.

Mandras later thanked Velisarios for firing at him as he came round the bend at the entrance to the village. But at the time he greatly disliked being carried in the arms of the strongman to the doctor's house and he did not enjoy having a bent nail removed from his shoulder. What he thanked Megalo Velisarios for was that in the doctor's house he first set eyes on Pelagia. There was a moment when he became aware that he was being bandaged, that a young woman's long hair was brushing against his face. He opened his eyes and found himself gazing into a pair of anxious eyes. 'At that moment,' he liked to say later, 'I recognized my future wife.'

◆

Dr Iannis put on a fresh shirt in readiness for his daily visit to the *kapheneion,** and stepped out into the yard. He was entirely unsurprised to see Mandras there, talking to Pelagia. The young fisherman's face went red when he saw him. 'Oh, good evening, doctor. I've brought you some fish,' he said.

The doctor twisted his mouth and pretended to sigh. 'Mandras,' he said, 'you know perfectly well that I know perfectly well that you have only come here to flirt with Pelagia.'

'Flirt?' repeated the young man, attempting to appear both innocent and shocked.

'Yes. Flirt. Yesterday you brought us another fish and then flirted with Pelagia for an hour. Well, you'd better get on with it.'

'Then I have your permission to talk to your daughter?'

'Talk, talk, talk,' said Dr Iannis, waving his hands, and he set off for the *kapheneion*.

'Your dad's a funny fellow,' Mandras said to Pelagia.

'There's nothing wrong with my father,' she exclaimed, 'and anyone who says there is gets a broom in the face.' She pushed the broom at him and he caught it and twisted it out of her grasp. 'Give it back,' she said laughing.

'I'll give it back . . . in return for a kiss.'

Pelagia gave the young man a flirtatious smile.

At the *kapheneion*, the doctor collected his tiny cup of coffee and sat next to Kokolios, as he always did. The coffee shop was

***

* *kapheneion*: the Greek word for a village coffee shop, where men drink coffee and chat.

full of the usual characters: the Communist* Kokolios, with his splendid moustache; old man Stamatis; Father Arsenios, round and sweating. 'What's the news of the war?' Kokolios asked.

The doctor twisted the ends of his moustache and said, 'Germany is taking everything, the Italians are behaving like fools, the French have run away, the Americans have been playing ball games, the British have been drinking tea, the Russians have been sitting on their hands. Thank God we are out of it. Why don't we turn on the radio?'

The large British radio in the corner of the room was switched on, its whistles reduced to a minimum by moving it around. Just then, Pelagia appeared at the door, gesturing urgently, greatly embarrassed by her presence in the men-only *kapheneion*. The doctor raised his eyes to the ceiling, put his pipe in his pocket and went to the door. 'What is it, girl?'

'It's Mandras, he's fallen out of a tree on to a pot.'

The doctor shook his head in disbelief and allowed his daughter to hurry him home. There, he made Mandras lie on the kitchen table while he removed tiny pieces of the broken pot from the young man's muscular back. 'You're a fool,' he told his patient.

'I know, doctor,' said Madras, biting his lip as another piece came out.

'Stop being so polite. I know what you're planning. Are you going to ask her to marry you or not?'

'Not yet, doctor. Everyone says there's going to be a war, and I don't want to leave a widow. You know how people treat a widow.'

'Quite right,' said the doctor and wondered, as he wiped away a spot of blood, whether his body had ever been as beautiful as this young fool's.

---

* Communist: a supporter of Communism, a political system based on the idea that people are equal and that things should not be privately owned.

It was several hours before he returned to the *kapheneion*. When he entered, he knew immediately that something was wrong. Warlike music came from the radio and Dr Iannis was astonished to see that the faces of several of the men were shiny with tears. 'What's going on?' he asked.

'Those Italian pigs have sunk one of our ships at Tinos. And they fired on the harbour there. It was full of people. On a holy day, too.'

The doctor put his hands to his face and felt his own tears fighting to appear. He was possessed by a feeling of helpless anger. He did not stop to question whether war with Italy was inevitable. Although he did not believe in God he found himself saying, 'Come on boys, we're all going to the church.' The men of the *kapheneion* rose and followed him.


## Chapter 2    Pelagia and Mandras

Pelagia (resting in the afternoon): *Papas*★ says that Mandras is going to have tiny pieces of that pot in his back for the rest of his life. I like his body, what I've seen of it. God forgive me, I have such wicked thoughts. Thank God no one can read my mind, or I'd be locked up and all the old women would throw stones at me. I wonder what Mandras is doing. He's so beautiful and so funny too. He made my stomach ache with laughing before he fell out of the tree. That's when I knew I loved him; it was the fear I felt when he fell on the pot.

When will he ask me to marry him? But he's not a serious fellow, and it gives me doubts. He's so funny, but I can't talk to him about anything and you have to be able to discuss things with a husband, don't you? I say, 'Is there going to be a war?' and

★ *Papas, Papakis*: Greek for *Dad, Daddy*.

he just grins and says, 'Who cares? Is there going to be a kiss?' I don't want there to be a war. Let there be Mandras standing in the yard with a fish in his hands. Let there be Mandras every day with a fish.

Mandras (leaving the harbour in his boat): It's going to be too hot again today, I know it, and all the fish will hide in the rocks and go to the bottom. Let the clouds hide the sun, let me catch some fine fish and I'll take one to Pelagia and she'll ask me to eat with them, and I can rub her leg with my foot under the table while the doctor discusses ancient poetry. I know he likes me, but he doesn't think I'm good enough for her – he's always calling me a fool.

The trouble is that I can't be myself when I'm with her. I mean, I am a serious man. I follow politics, I want to improve the world. But when I'm with Pelagia it's as if I'm twelve again. I want to amuse her and what else am I supposed to do? I can't imagine myself saying, 'Come on, Pelagia, let's talk about politics.' Women aren't interested in that sort of thing, they want you to entertain them. Perhaps *she* thinks I'm a fool as well. I'm not in her class, I know that. The doctor taught her Italian and a bit of English, and they're not a typical island family. I mean, the doctor's sailed all over the world, he's even been to America. And where have I been? What do I know? I love Pelagia, but I know that I will never be a man until I've done something important, something people can respect me for. I feel so useless and insignificant here on the island.

Pelagia (taking roast lamb from the village oven): Where is Mandras? He's usually here by now. I want him to come, I can hardly breathe, I want him so much. My hands are shaking again. I'd better take this silly smile off my face or everyone will think I'm mad. Come, Mandras, please come, stay for dinner and stroke my ankles with your feet, Mandras.

Mandras (mending his nets): We're going to go to war with

Italy very soon. I've got a letter saying that I'll be ordered to join the army in the next few weeks. I know one thing, I'm going to ask Pelagia to marry me before I leave. With no jokes. I'm going to make her understand that in defending Greece I'm defending her and every woman like her, and if I die, I'll die with the name of Pelagia and the name of Greece equally on my lips. And if I live, I'll walk with my head held high for the rest of my life, and everyone will say, 'That's Mandras, who fought in the war. We owe everything to people like him.'

◆

The island's saint, St Geronimos, dead for five centuries, had lived a genuinely holy life and had left his ancient blackened body in an island church as evidence of this. He was so loved by the islanders that he had two feast days, one in August and another in October, and on these days he tolerantly looked elsewhere as the population of the island became excessively drunk. It was eight days before Greece and Italy declared war on each other, but it might have been any October feast day in the last hundred years. The cruelty had gone out of the sun, and the delightfully warm day was made even more pleasant by a light wind from the sea that wandered in and out of the trees. From all over the island, people made their way to the church where the saint's body lay, packing the church tightly and squeezing together in the yard outside. At different points in the crowd, Velisarios, Pelagia, Dr Iannis, Kokolios and Stamatis all turned their heads sideways to hear the distant prayers of the priest. The sun climbed higher and the people, packed together, began to sweat. The heat was just becoming unbearable when the service ended, the bells rang out and the celebrations began.

A small band began playing while a line of pretty girls stepped from side to side at the back, and a row of young men danced with their heads twisted backwards. Those who were drunk began to insult each other, and in some places fighting had already begun. Pelagia moved nearer the church and sat on a bench. Someone tapped on her shoulder and she looked up and saw Mandras. He fell drunkenly to his knees and declared dramatically, 'Pelagia, will you marry me? Marry me or I die!'

She regarded him silently for a moment, then said quietly, 'Of course I'll marry you.' When he heard this, Mandras leapt joyfully but unsteadily into the air, then suddenly became extremely serious and said, 'My darling, I love you with all my heart, but we can't get married until I get back from the Army.'

'Go and speak to my father,' said Pelagia. Then, worried by the strange way in which she did not feel as happy as she ought, she made her way back to the church in order to be alone with the saint. Time passed, and Mandras failed to find the doctor before drink overcame him. He slept sweetly in a pool of something disgusting but unidentifiable, while, nearby, Lemoni attempted to set fire to the beard of the sleeping Father Arsenios, and Kokolios and Stamatis became lost in the bushes while searching for their wives.

Pelagia walked back from the feast with her father, bursting with a painful mixture of anxiety and happiness, desperate to mention Mandras's proposal. But the doctor was in a much too drunken state to be sensitive to his daughter's feelings, and when they reached the house, he danced about the yard before falling onto his bed fully clothed.

Pelagia went to bed and could not sleep. 'I love you, Mandras,' she declared, at the same time as doubts rose in her like an invasion of tiny devils. How much did she really know Mandras? What evidence did she have that he was patient and kind? Can you trust someone who replies immediately, without thought? She was frightened by the suspicion that there was something hard about his heart. If it were not love that she felt for Mandras, then why this breathlessness, this endless desire

11

that made her heart beat fast? She imagined that Mandras had died, and as the tears came she was shocked to discover that she also felt relief.

In the morning she took herself to the yard and created tasks that would cause her to see him as soon as he came around the curve of the road. But he did not come, and Pelagia passed the day with feelings of impatience that soon turned into real concern. That evening, when he had still not appeared, her father said, quite unexpectedly, 'I expect he hasn't come because he's feeling as sick as everyone else.'

Pelagia took his hand and kissed it gratefully. 'He's asked me to marry him. I told him I'd have to ask you,' she said.

'I don't want to marry Mandras,' said Dr Iannis. 'It would be a much better idea if he married you, I think.'

'Don't you approve of him, *Papakis*?'

He turned and looked at her gently. 'He's too young. Also, I have not done you a favour. You read poetry, you speak Italian. He isn't your equal, and he would expect to be better than his wife. He is a man, after all. I have often thought that you would only ever be able to marry happily with a foreigner, a dentist from Norway or something.'

Pelagia laughed at the ridiculous thought, then closed her eyes. The doctor went inside and came out with something that he handed very formally to her. She took it, saw what it was, and dropped it into her skirts with a cry of horror.

The doctor remained standing. 'There's going to be a war, and terrible things happen in wars, especially to women. Use the gun to defend yourself. It might happen that your marriage will have to wait. We must make sure first that Mussolini does not invite himself to the wedding.' He turned and went into the house, leaving Pelagia to her fears, and after a few minutes she went to her room and placed the gun under her pillow, imagining once again that Mandras was dead.

12

It was not until the third day after the feast that there was a quiet knock at the door. Mandras stood, speaking fast, a bucket of fish in his hand. 'I'm sorry I didn't come sooner, but I was ill the day after the feast, and yesterday I had to collect my Army papers, and I'm leaving for Athens the day after tomorrow, and I've spoken to your father, and he's agreed to the marriage, and I've brought you some fish.'

Pelagia sat on her bed and went cold inside; it was too much happiness, too much pain. She was engaged to a man who mixed marriage together with fish and war, a man who was too beautiful to go away and die in the snows of Tsamoria. Suddenly Mandras seemed to her to be an extraordinarily delicate creature, so delicate and beautiful that he was sure to die. Her hands began to shake and she whispered, 'Don't go, don't go.'

## Chapter 3   The Homosexual

I, Carlo Piero Guercio, write these words with the intention that they should be found after my death, when what is written here will not harm me.

I know only silence. I have not told the priest, since I know in advance what I will be told; it is a wicked sin and I must marry and lead the life of a normal man. Nor have I told a doctor, as I know that I will be informed that I am sick and can be cured of my disease.

What could I say to such priests and doctors? I would say to the priest that God made me like this for a purpose, that I had no choice. I would say to the doctor, 'I have been like this from the start, it is nature that has created me.' But they would not understand. I am like someone who is the only person in the world that knows the truth, but is forbidden to speak. And this

13

truth weighs more than the universe, this burden cracks my bones.

In my search to understand myself, I have read everything, from the most modern to the most ancient, and it was in the work of the ancient Greek philosopher, Plato, that I finally found myself. In his writings, he explained that there were three sexes, the third sex being men who loved men, and this idea made sense to me. Plato also wrote that if an army was made up of men who loved one another, they would be the bravest army in the world, because men would become heroes, ready to die for their lovers.

I admit that I joined the Army because the men are young and beautiful, and because I knew that in the Army I would find someone I could love though never touch. I would not abandon him in battle, I would win his admiration, I would die for him if necessary and in this way give purpose to my life.

In the Army I found my family. It was a world without women, and for the first time in my life I did not have to pretend. I was very fortunate at first; our unit was sent to Albania, where there was no real fighting, and we did not realize that we might be ordered to invade Greece. No one outside the Army can understand the joy of being a soldier, of being part of a group where you are all young and strong and quickly learn everything about each other. We believed we could not die, we could march eighty kilometres a day, singing battle songs. We were new and beautiful, we loved each other more than brothers.

I fell in love with Francesco, a young married soldier from Genoa, who accepted me as his best friend without ever suspecting my passion for him. He was an entirely beautiful boy, reminding me of one of those elegant cats that give the impression of immense but easy strength. I was attracted most of all to his face, with its strong, high cheekbones, wide mouth and one-sided smile. He was always amusing and respected no one, constantly entertaining us with his wickedly accurate imitations of Mussolini* and Hitler†. Everyone loved him, he never got a promotion and he did not care.

We soldiers loved the army life but had no love of the Fascist leaders of our country, nor did we have any idea of why we were in Albania. However, looking back, it seems clear that an invasion of Greece must have been the final intention; there were clues everywhere, if only we had seen them. In the first place, there was the fact that all the roads that we built (which, we were informed, were for the benefit of the Albanians) led towards the Greek border. In the second place, we heard stories from reliable sources about how our frontier posts were attacked a number of times by our own people dressed as Greeks, so that we could blame the latter for the attacks. When some Albanians shot at our soldiers, we announced that our attackers were Greeks. We also learned that one of our leaders arranged to have his own offices blown up so that Mussolini could finally declare war against the Greeks.

I have related these things as if they were amusing, but really they were acts of madness. When war against Greece was finally declared, we were told that the Greeks would be defeated within days. We were sent off to die, with no transport, no equipment and too few men. At first, having no idea of what the future held for us, we whistled and sang, and from time to time Francesco, marching beside me, looked at me and smiled. 'Athens in two weeks,' he said.

Then the weather turned against us and rain poured from the skies, turning the ground to mud so that we struggled through it, ten thousand men whose uniforms were weighted down with

---

* Mussolini: Fascist leader of Italy who ruled from 1922–43. Fascism is a political system in which people's lives are completely controlled by the state.

† Hitler: Fascist leader of Germany from 1934–45. He led Germany in the Second World War.

water, our aeroplanes unable to fly because of the bad weather. Our twenty heavy guns sank into the mud, and our animals were unable to pull them out. We struggled on in these conditions for several days, at a height of three hundred metres, our legs turned to ice so that we could no longer feel our feet. 'Athens in two months,' said Francesco with a twisted smile. But we saw no sign of the Greeks and believed that we were winning without fighting.

On 1 November, a bomb fell among us and there was a scream as a poor fellow from Piedmont lost his legs, followed by the short, sharp sound of gunshot from the trees. We realized that the Greeks had cleverly got us into a position where we could be surrounded and cut off from all help. We were trapped in the valley floor and the Greeks, whom we very rarely saw, moved like ghosts among the upper slopes, so that we never knew when we would be attacked or from where. Their bombs seemed at one moment to come from behind, at another moment to come from the side or from the front. We fired at ghosts and at mountain goats. The heroic Greeks seemed to rise out of the ground and fall on us as if we had raped their mothers. It shocked us. We had no air support. 'Athens in two years,' said Francesco. We were completely alone.

We ate only dry biscuits, but when our horses died, we ate them. We were ordered to turn back and had to fight our way through the soldiers that surrounded us. We grew immense beards, we were half buried in snowstorms, our red, swollen eyes sank deep into our heads, our hands were torn as if by cats. We became desperately thin, digging for food in the frozen ground like pigs. It was a hell of machine guns, bombs and ice, a hell in which battles were fought without rest for eight hours at a time, while on the mountains our dead lay in forgotten piles, body upon body. We fought on but we lost our hearts as a great darkness settled across the land. The snow fell endlessly. My boots, crawling with insects, fell apart. I think it must have been December when we understood that we were as broken as our boots.

Waking up in the morning, ten degrees below zero. The first question: who has frozen to death now? Who has slipped from sleep to death? These were the days of the white death, in which the legs became swollen and turned bright purple, deep blue, coal black. I was exhausted, shaken by the screams of men in unimaginable pain as their legs were cut off by our army doctors. I lived in fear of the white death and inspected my feet every few hours. Francesco was undoubtedly mad. His mouth moved continually, his beard became a column of ice, his eyes rolled in his head and he did not recognize me. We had lost four thousand men. There was nothing in our lives except the white death, the bitter absence of our friends, the joylessness of the icy mountains.

One morning Francesco turned to me with a wild expression in his eyes, speaking to me for the first time in weeks. 'Look,' he said and rolled up his trousers, revealing the purple stripes on the white flesh. He touched the dead flesh with a look of horror in his eyes, rolled his trousers back down again and said to me, 'It's enough, Carlo. It's too much.' He began to weep, trembling all over. Then he took up his gun and, before I could prevent him, advanced towards the enemy, stopping to fire every five steps. In recognition of his heroism, the Greeks did not return his fire, but a bomb fell next to him and he disappeared beneath a shower of mud. There was a long silence. I saw something move where Francesco had been.

I put my gun down and ran towards the place where he lay. The Greeks did not shoot at me and I saw that although the side of his head had been blown away, he was still alive. I knelt and gathered him into my arms, then stood up and faced the Greeks, offering myself to their guns. There was a silence, and then a

17

cheer came from them. I turned and carried the bleeding bundle back to our side.

Francesco took two hours to die. His blood ran down my uniform, his mouth formed silent words, the light in his eyes faded and he began the long, slow journey towards death, suffering what must have been indescribable pain. I buried him in a deep hole, the home of enormous rats.

We lost the war and were saved only when the Germans invaded from Bulgaria, forcing the Greeks to fight two different armies at the same time. We fought and froze and died for no purpose. I took no part in the shameful conquest of Greece because the day after I buried Francesco, I shot myself in the flesh of my thigh.


## Chapter 4    The Wild Man

On 28 October, Greece and Italy formally declared war on each other. All the young men of Cephallonia disappeared to join the army, and Dr Iannis attempted to join too but was turned down when it was discovered that he had learned all his medical knowledge on ships and had no proper qualifications. Several Italian families on the island were attacked and their houses were burnt down, and the islanders developed a silent, sorrowful expression as they learnt to live with the thought that their sons and brothers might die. As the weeks passed, however, they were comforted by the news that their country was winning the war and that the Greeks were winning back territory that was theirs by right in Albania. The villagers went often to church and Father Arsenios surprised them by making fine, emotional speeches and by not getting drunk. Almost immediately, shortages of certain foods and other household essentials developed, and beans became the greater part of the doctor's and Pelagia's diet.

The war had the effect of increasing the importance of Dr Iannis, as the village community turned to him for advice and leadership. The doctor watched his daughter progress through a series of emotions, all of which seemed to him to be unhealthy and worrying. At first Pelagia had been in a state of painful anxiety, and then in storms of tears. She would sit by the wall outside as if she expected her fiancé to arrive at the bend of the road where he had been shot by Velisarios. Later, she developed the habit of remaining silently in the room with her father, her hands motionless in her lap as tears followed each other silently down her cheeks. Pelagia calmed her fears by writing letter after letter to Mandras, relating island news and gossip, telling him about her terrible dreams and her fears for him, and begging him to write back to her. She began the task of making a cover for their marriage bed, but lacked the benefit of a mother's instruction in such matters. Each time it reached a certain stage, it began to look suspiciously like a dead animal, and she felt forced to undo her work and begin again.

As day followed day it became clear that not only had Mandras not written, but that he never would. After careful observation of his daughter, her father realized that she was becoming bitter and increasingly certain that her fiancé could not love her. When he realized that Pelagia was seriously depressed, the doctor made her accompany him on his medical visits, sent her to bed early and let her sleep in the mornings. He made a habit of making her laugh against her will, and deliberately made her angry by such tricks as moving all the knives from one drawer to another. The doctor considered the return of her normal cheerful manner to be a sign that she had given up her passion for Mandras. On the one hand, he was glad of this, since he did not truly believe that Mandras would make a good husband, but on the other hand, Pelagia was already engaged, and the breaking of an engagement would cause great shame. The awful possibility occurred to him that Pelagia might marry a man she no longer loved out of a sense of duty.

♦

Pelagia returned from the village with a jar of water upon her shoulder, set it down in the yard and came through the door, singing. The news had been bad for some weeks – not only had Kokolios lost two of his sons, but the Germans had attacked the Greek army so that the courageous Greek troops were at last facing defeat. Strangely, the bad news made Pelagia even more appreciative of the first signs of spring on the island. She was feeling strong and whole and was enjoying having the house to herself while her father was away visiting a friend on the other side of the island.

Pelagia's singing was brought to a sudden stop when she entered the kitchen. There was a stranger seated at the kitchen table, a most wild and horrible stranger, whose hands trembled ceaselessly and whose head was utterly hidden beneath a mass of dirt, mud and hair. An enormous beard hid the lower half of the stranger's face, in which Pelagia could see only two tiny bright eyes that would not look at her. Rags covered the stranger's body and in the place of shoes there were bandages, stained with blood both old and new.

Overcome with fear and pity, not knowing what to do, Pelagia said, 'My father's out. He should be back tomorrow.'

'You're happy, anyway. Singing,' said the man in a cracked voice, and his whole body shook.

'You can't stay, I'm on my own,' said Pelagia.

'I can't walk,' replied the man. 'I walked from Epirus. No boots.' Just then, the goat wandered through the open kitchen door, approached the stranger and made a gentle attempt at tasting the stranger's rags. 'Ah, at least your goat remembers me,' the man whispered, and began to weep.

Pelagia was astonished by these words and said, 'Mandras?'

The man turned his face towards her and said, 'Don't touch me, Pelagia. There are insects crawling all over me and I smell terrible.'

Pelagia felt guilt, pity, disgust. It seemed unimaginable that this pitiful ghost hid the mind and body of the man she loved. 'You never wrote to me,' she said, making the accusation that had destroyed her love for him and left her empty.

Mandras replied, 'I can't write.' For a reason she did not understand, Pelagia was more disgusted by this confession than by Mandras's physical condition. 'Couldn't someone else have written for you? I thought you were dead. I thought you . . . couldn't love me.'

'How could I let everyone know? How could I have my feelings discussed by the boys?' He glanced up again so that at last she recognized his eyes, and said, 'Pelagia, I got all your letters. I couldn't read them but I got them.' From inside his clothing he drew out a huge, dirty packet. 'I carried you in here,' he said, beating his chest. 'Every day, all the time, I was thinking of you, talking to you. I was not a coward because of you, I even prayed to you. And when the Germans attacked us I got through their lines, and all I could think of was that I had to get home to you, and now . . .' His body shook as he wept. 'Now only the animals know me.'

'I'll fetch your mother,' Pelagia whispered and ran out of the house, down to the small, fishy but extremely clean house by the harbour where *Kyria** Drosoula, Mandras's widowed mother, lived. *Kyria* Drosoula was a woman so large and ugly that at their first meeting people wondered how she had ever found a husband. She was in fact a brave, kind woman, and during Mandras's absence she and Pelagia had comforted one another.

* *Kyria*: Greek for *Mrs* or *Miss*.

Now the two women returned, breathless, to the doctor's house, and found Mandras in exactly the same position that Pelagia had left him in.

Drosoula ran into the kitchen with a cry of joy and then stepped back with an astonished look that in other circumstances would have been amusing. 'It is him,' said Pelagia. 'I told you he was in an awful state.'

'My God,' Drosoula exclaimed, then began to inspect Mandras as if he were an animal she was considering purchasing. 'Go and put a big pot to boil,' she said finally, 'because I'm going to wash him from head to foot, but first I'm going to get rid of this hair, so bring me some scissors.'

Mandras sat motionless as his mother, making terrible faces as she did so, cut away the ropes and lumps of his hair and beard, revealing the horribly infected state of the skin below and the insects creeping all over it. Pelagia felt sickened where she knew that she should feel pity, and went indoors to look in her father's medicine cupboard. She realized with a small shock that she had learned enough from her father over the years to become a doctor herself. Hurrying outside, she told Drosoula which treatments to use on Mandras's face and head and where to use them. After a brief discussion about whether it was correct for a woman to see her fiancé with nothing on, the two women decided that in these circumstances it was entirely acceptable.

They removed Mandras's rags, and after gazing sorrowfully at the parcel of skin and bones that sat before them, again under Pelagia's expert guidance, Drosoula began washing her son and rubbing healing oils and creams on him. Pelagia forced herself to remove the bandages from Mandras's feet, and despite the fact that at first sight they did not look as if they could be saved, on closer examination she realized that the flesh was quite dry. She fetched a bowl of clean water, salted it heavily, and as gently as she could, she washed and treated the terrible mess.

When Dr Iannis returned the following morning, he found not only a half-dead man asleep in his daughter's bed, but his daughter and an amazingly ugly woman asleep in his own. He listened to Pelagia's account of everything she had done, then examined the patient carefully, paying particular attention to the feet. Pelagia nervously waited for his anger. 'Well done, I have never been so proud,' he declared. Drosoula smiled at Pelagia, who was so relieved that her hands were shaking, and the two women made more plans for Mandras's recovery.

## Chapter 5    30 April 1941: Invasion

Though he said little, being almost incapable of speech due to his physical condition, Mandras was fully aware of the change in Pelagia's attitude towards him and he hated the way in which his mother and fiancée had undressed him, washed him and discussed him as if he were not present. But the horrors of war and starvation had taken away from him the will to live, so that he lay for weeks in bed in his mother's house, incapable of moving or even speaking, constantly revisiting in his mind the terrible experiences that had been his.

The brilliance of his Greek leaders had enabled him and many of his companions to survive the war against the Italians, but the freezing conditions in the mountains and lack of food meant that his body aged more in a few months than it would normally do in sixty years. Then, when the Germans had attacked from the south, Mandras's unit had marched back down into Greece and had fought bravely but uselessly against their enemy, leaving Mandras the only survivor in his unit. With a vision of a loving, smiling Pelagia constantly before him, Mandras had found the strength to struggle home, wearing bandages instead of boots, through the wild hills, mountains and forests that made up the greater part of Greece.

For much of his journey he had met very few people and had consequently almost died from starvation. If he had been met on his return to Cephallonia by the loving Pelagia of his dreams, Mandras's recovery might have been faster. But as week followed week, Pelagia, though she tried hard to love Mandras, felt only coldness towards him, coldness and the growing conviction that Mandras was remaining ill in order to punish her for her lack of warmth towards him.

'He thinks that nobody wants him,' said Dr Iannis, 'and he's doing this in order to force us to show him that we do.'

'But I don't want him,' thought Pelagia, again and again, as she sat making the bedcover that had never grown beyond the size of a towel. But although she spent a lot of time either with or thinking about Mandras, there were other matters that occupied her mind just as much. By April 1941, the German army had reached Athens, and the royal palace there was occupied not by King George of Greece but by German soldiers. On the 28th of the month, the Italian army, claiming that the Ionian islands belonged to them by right, invaded the island of Corfu, making it inevitable that Cephallonia would be next on the list.

For the islanders, the waiting was painful. Every last moment of freedom and security was rolled about on the tongue, tasted and remembered. Fathers who expected to be beaten to death stroked the hair of pretty daughters who expected to be raped. Sons sat with their mothers on doorsteps and talked gently of their memories. Father Arsenios knelt in his church, attempting to find words to a prayer, puzzled by an odd sensation of having been abandoned by God instead of the other way round.

In these last weeks before the invasion, Dr Iannis wrote what he believed to be the final part of his 'History of Cephallonia':

'Among those who invaded and occupied our island – the Romans, the Turks, the Russians, the French, the British' – he began, 'the Italians made the greatest impression upon us, because

24

we spent the period from 1194 to 1797 under Italian rule. This explains a great many things that may puzzle the foreigner, for example, the numerous Italian words that exist in our vocabulary, and the architecture of the island, which is almost entirely Italian.'

He continued on this subject for a number of pages, then, when it seemed that the Italian invasion was due at any moment, he wrote:

'I wait in the knowledge that this may be the last thing I ever write. I beg that whoever finds these papers should preserve and not destroy them.'

Placing the papers in a black tin box, the doctor lifted the old carpet beneath the table and opened a trapdoor, revealing the large hole that had been made in 1849 in order to hide island rebels sought by the British, who then governed the island. He placed his work safely inside the hole, then went outside to listen for the sound of approaching aeroplanes.

On 30 April foreign aircraft and ships were seen approaching from the horizon. Drosoula ran inside to Pelagia shouting, 'Italians, Italians. It's the invasion.'

Pelagia's immediate reaction was to run up the hill to be with her father, whom she found standing in his doorway, as everyone else stood in theirs, protecting his eyes against the sun as he watched the planes. Out of breath, she flew into his arms and felt him tremble, then realized with a small shock that he shook, not from fear, but from excitement.

'History,' he cried, 'all this time I have been writing history, and now history is happening before my eyes.'

The Italian soldiers stepped apologetically out of their aircraft and ships and waved cheerfully but hesitantly to the people in their doorways. In the village, Pelagia and her father watched the Italian units go by, their leaders consulting maps with puzzled faces. A line of men marched by, led by Captain Antonio Corelli, with the mandolin that he had named Antonia hanging on his back. When he saw Pelagia he shouted, '*Bella bambina*,★ eyes left!'

The heads of the soldiers turned in her direction, and for one unbelievable minute Pelagia was forced to watch the most ridiculous behaviour. There was a soldier who crossed his eyes and folded down his lower lip, another who pushed his lips out and blew her a kiss, another who pretended at each step to stumble over his own feet. Pelagia put her hand to her mouth. 'Don't laugh,' ordered the doctor. 'It's our duty to hate them.'

All over Cephallonia the islanders painted rude remarks about the invaders in huge letters on all available walls. The men related Italian jokes. What is the shortest book in the world? *The Italian Book of War Heroes.* Why do Italians wear moustaches? To be reminded of their mothers. A decision was made that the local population should provide Italian officers with accommodation. So one day the doctor came home and found a round Italian officer standing in the kitchen.

'*Buon giorno*,'★ said the officer.

'*Buon giorno*,' the doctor replied. 'Perhaps you could tell me why you are here.'

'Ah,' said the man uncomfortably, 'I am sorry to say, you are going to have to provide accommodation for an officer.'

'Impossible,' said the doctor angrily. Then an interesting thought occurred to him and he asked, 'Do you have a supply of medicines?'

'Naturally,' replied the officer. The two men exchanged glances, understanding perfectly what the other was thinking.

'There are many things I need,' said the doctor.

'And I need accommodation. So?'

'So it's a deal,' said the doctor.

'A deal,' repeated the officer. 'Anything you want, send me a message through Captain Corelli. You will find him charming.'

★ *Bella bambina, buon giorno*: Italian for *beautiful girl* and *good day*.

In the early evening Captain Corelli arrived, driven by another soldier, Carlo Piero Guercio. The captain looked around, appreciating the signs of a quiet domestic life. There was a goat tied to a tree, and a young woman with dark eyes at a table, with a scarf tied round her head and a large cooking knife in her hand. The captain fell to his knees before her and exclaimed dramatically, 'Please don't kill me, I am innocent.'

Pelagia smiled, against her will, and glanced at Carlo, amazed to see that he was as big as Velisarios. The captain leapt up. 'I am Captain Antonio Corelli and this . . .' he took Carlo by the arm, '. . . is one of our heroes. He rescued a fallen friend under fire.'

'It's nothing,' said Carlo with a shy smile, and Pelagia knew immediately that, despite his size, he was a soft and saddened man. 'This . . .' Corelli continued, tapping a case in his hand, '. . . is Antonia. By what name do men know you, may I ask?'

Pelagia looked at Corelli properly for the first time and realized that this was the same officer who had commanded his men to march past at 'eyes left'. At the same moment Corelli recognized her. 'Ah,' he exclaimed and smacked himself on the wrist, then fell to his knees once more and said softly, 'Forgive me, I have sinned.'

Dr Iannis came out, saw the captain on his knees and said, 'Captain Corelli? I want a word with you. Now.'

Surprised by the authority in the older man's voice, Corelli stood up and held out his hand, but the doctor did not put out his own, instead saying sharply, 'I want an explanation please. Why has the teaching of Greek history been forbidden in schools? And why is everyone being forced to learn Italian?'

The captain felt himself wanting to run away like a little boy. 'I am not responsible for it,' he said.

The doctor frowned fiercely and shook his finger at the captain. 'There would be no wars, captain, if men like you took more responsibility.'

27

'I must protest,' the captain replied weakly.

'Fool,' said the doctor forcefully and returned inside, very satisfied with himself. Pelagia could not help feeling sorry for the captain. 'Your father is . . .' he said, and the words failed him.

'Yes, he is,' confirmed Pelagia.

'Where shall I sleep?' asked Corelli, eager to change the subject.

'You will have my bed,' said Pelagia.

Under normal circumstances Antonio Corelli would have asked brightly, 'Are we going to share it then? How kind,' but now, after the doctor's words, he received this information with horror. 'Impossible,' he said. 'Tonight I shall sleep in the yard and tomorrow I shall request alternative accommodation.'

Pelagia was shocked by the feelings of anxiety that rose in her. Could there be something inside her that wanted this foreigner, this invader, to stay? She went inside and told her father about the captain's decision. 'He can't go,' he said. 'How am I supposed to be nasty to him if he isn't here? And anyway, he seems like a pleasant boy.' He took his daughter's arm and went back out with her. 'Young man,' he said to the captain, 'you are staying here whether you like it or not. It is quite possible that we will be sent someone even worse.'

'Yes,' said the captain, overcome with embarrassment.

'*Kyria* Pelagia will bring water, some coffee and food. You will find we look after our guests, even those who do not deserve it. Your vast friend is welcome to join us.'

The captain went to call Carlo to the meal in a state of miserable obedience and utter defeat.

When the captain woke after his first night in the doctor's house, he went into the kitchen, saw Pelagia fast asleep and did not know what to do. He looked down upon her and realized he wanted to crawl in beside her – nothing could have seemed more natural – but instead he returned to his room and took his mandolin, Antonia, out of its case. After practising for five minutes or so, he began playing a very fast, complicated piece, forgetful of the sleeping girl next door, so that Pelagia woke to indescribably beautiful music coming from somewhere in the house. She lay listening, then went to dress in her father's room, and Corelli, realizing that she had risen at last, came out into the kitchen.

'That was lovely,' commented Pelagia.

He looked unhappy. 'I'm sorry, I woke you up.'

'That's very beautiful,' she said, gesturing towards the instrument. 'Why do you play the mandolin?'

'Why does one do anything? My uncle gave me Antonia and I discovered I could be a good musician. When the war's over, I'm going to become a professional concert player and composer.'

'You're going to be rich and famous, then,' Pelagia said jokingly. 'Why don't you play me something?'

The captain picked up the mandolin, and a stream of notes poured from it that made Pelagia's mouth fall open. She had never before heard such complex, lovely music. She realized for the first time that music was not just a sweet sound, but was, to those who understood it, an emotional and intellectual journey, a journey that she wanted to share. She leaned forward and put her hands together as if she were at prayer.

'There you are,' said the captain when he had finished.

In her excitement at the music, she wanted to dance and spin round, but she only said, 'I just don't understand why an artist like you would descend to being a soldier. It's a waste of time.'

'Of course it's a waste of time.' He rose and glanced at his watch. 'Carlo should have been here by now. I'll have to go and find him.' He looked at her with one eyebrow raised and said, 'By the way, Signorina, I couldn't help noticing that you have a gun in the pocket of your skirt.'

Pelagia began to tremble but the captain continued, 'I understand why you might want to have it, and in fact I haven't

29

seen it at all, but you must realize what would happen if someone else saw it. Be more careful.'

She looked up at him, appealing with her eyes, and he smiled, tapped the side of his nose and was gone.

◆

Carlo had not arrived with the car to pick up Captain Corelli, because it had broken down some kilometres from the village. After kicking the car a number of times, Carlo had set off on foot towards the village. Velisarios passed him and the two men looked at one another with something like recognition, because both men had become accustomed to the sad suspicion that they were unique in a peculiar way. They were both amazed at the other's size and for a moment forgot that they were enemies. 'Hey!' said Velisarios, raising his hands in a gesture of pleasure. Carlo offered him one of his disgusting cigarettes, Velisarios accepted, and they made sour faces to each other as they smoked. They then went their separate ways, more content than before they had met.

As Carlo walked up the hill towards the house, his mind turned towards Captain Corelli. For the first time since the death of Francesco in the mountains of Albania, the soldier was experiencing a kind of happiness; in the captain he had once again found a man whom he could love and serve. In his eyes, Corelli was endlessly optimistic, a clear fountain, a kind of saint who remained a man of honour because he knew no other way to be. Carlo knew that some people thought that Corelli was a little mad, but for him, the captain was a man who loved life so much that he did not care what kind of an impression he made.

One of the pleasures of Carlo's life, at that time, was an opera group called La Scala that the captain had organized from among those of his men who could sing. Carlo, who had a fine singing voice, had been invited to join when the captain had heard him singing as he polished his boots. There was another more unusual member of the opera group, a young German soldier called Günter Weber, part of a troop of three thousand German soldiers who had accompanied the Italian army on their invasion of the island. Although relations between the Germans and Italians appeared friendly, the Germans thought of the Italians as inferior, and the Italians were puzzled by German discipline and lack of humour.

But Captain Corelli had made friends with Günter Weber, a boy who spoke some Italian and whom the captain liked because his face was open and friendly, and because when he got drunk he laughed and lost his German seriousness. Weber became a member of the opera club despite the fact that he could not sing a note. Neither Corelli nor Carlo knew that one day the German would betray his friends with a storm of bullets that would open red and bleeding wounds in the bodies of the companions he had grown to love.

## Chapter 6   The Freedom Fighter

After Captain Corelli had left, Pelagia did some household tasks, then went outside to brush her goat, thinking about the captain as she did so. Mandras caught her dreaming.

He had climbed out of bed, cursing and completely cured, on the day of the invasion, as if the arrival of the Italians was something so important that illness was a luxury to be left behind. He had gone down to the sea and swum as if he had never been away, and had returned with a smile on his face and a fish for Pelagia. But Pelagia only felt guilty now, whenever she saw him, and deeply uncomfortable.

She jumped when he tapped her on the shoulder and despite her effort to force a bright smile, he did not fail to see the look of alarm in her eyes. He ignored it but would remember it later. 'I'm going to join the freedom fighters,' he said. 'I'm leaving tomorrow.'

'Oh,' said Pelagia. There was a long silence, then she said, 'I won't be able to write.'

'I know.'

Pelagia shook her head slowly and sighed. 'Promise me one thing. Whenever you are planning to do something terrible, think of me and don't do it.'

'I'm a Greek,' he said gently. 'Not a Fascist. And I will think of you every minute.'

She heard the sincerity in his voice and felt herself wanting to cry. They embraced, like brother and sister, not people who were engaged to be married. 'God go with you,' said Pelagia, and he smiled sadly. 'And with you.'

'I shall always remember you swinging in the tree.'

They laughed, then he looked at her lovingly for one last moment, took a few steps, paused, turned and said softly, 'I shall always love you.'

♦

Mandras joined a group of three men in the hills of the *Peloponnisos* in southern Greece. They had neither plan nor purpose. All they knew was that they were driven by something from the depths of the soul, something that commanded them to rid their land of strangers or die in the attempt. They set fire to lorries, and one of their number stabbed an enemy soldier and afterwards sat shaking with fear and disgust while the others comforted and praised him. They lived on the edge of a forest in a cave, living off supplies brought by the priest of a neighbouring village. There were several other groups of freedom fighters in the area, the most organized being a Communist group known as ELAS (although it did not declare itself as communist, preferring to disguise the fact).

Mandras joined ELAS at first because he had no choice. He and his companions were lying in a small leafy shelter that they had built, when they were suddenly surrounded by ten men with thick beards, pointing guns at them. Their leader, who wore a dirty red cap, said, 'Come out,' and the men slowly stood up and came out, fearing for their lives, their hands upon the backs of their heads.

'Who are you with?' demanded the man with the cap.

'With no one,' replied Mandras, confused.

'The deal is that either you go back to your villages and leave us your weapons,' said the leader commandingly, 'or you fight us and we kill you, or you join us under my command. This is my territory and no one else's. Which is it?'

'We came to fight,' explained Mandras. 'Who are you?'

'I am Hector, not my real name, and we are the local branch of ELAS.' Hector's men grinned in a very friendly fashion, and Mandras looked from one of his companions to the others. 'We stay?' he asked, and they nodded. They had been too long in the hills to give up the fight and it was good to have found a leader who might know what ought to be done.

'Good,' said Hector. 'Come with us, and let's see what you are made of.'

He led Mandras and his companions three kilometres to a tiny house guarded by one of Hector's men. 'Bring him out,' Hector said, and the man kicked and pushed a thin old man out into the sunlight, where he stood trembling and blinking. Hector handed Mandras a length of knotted rope and, pointing to the old man, said, 'Beat him.'

Mandras stared at Hector in disbelief and the latter stared fiercely back at him. 'If you want to be with us, you've got to learn to teach these people a lesson. This man has been found guilty. Now beat him.'

Mandras struck the man once with the rope, lightly, because of the man's age, and Hector impatiently exclaimed, 'Harder, harder. What are you? A woman?' Mandras struck the old man once more, a little harder. 'Again,' commanded Hector.

It was easier each time he hit him. In fact it became a pleasure. It was as if all the anger from the earliest years of his childhood rose in him and was given expression. The old man threw himself to the ground, screaming, and Mandras suddenly knew he could be a god. Hector stepped forward, took the rope from his hand, and placed a gun in his grasp. 'Now kill him.'

Mandras knelt down and placed the gun against the old man's head, but he could not do it. He closed his eyes tight and told himself that he had to be a man in front of other men. Anyway, he was only doing what Hector had ordered him to do. The man was going to die anyway. Mandras tightened the muscles of his face and shot the man in the head.

Afterwards he looked not at the bloody mess of bone and brain, but in disbelief at the smoking gun. Hector patted Mandras on the back and said, 'Well done'. Mandras tried to struggle to his feet but could not do so, and Hector helped him up. 'Revolutionary justice,' he said. 'Historical necessity.'

As they left the village, Mandras found that he could not look anyone in the face and he stared down into the dirt. 'What did he do?' he asked finally.

'He was a dirty old thief. He took a bottle of whisky from supplies that were meant for us. You have to be tough with these people or they start doing what they like. They're full of the wrong ideas and it's just something we have to get out of them.'

◆

During his time with Hector, Mandras learnt a great many things. Hector taught Mandras to read and write, and taught him all about Communism. Mandras learnt that he was not a fisherman but a worker, and that he was as good as Dr Iannis and deserved the same pay. He learnt to take food and animals from hungry villagers without payment, since ELAS was working so hard on behalf of the Greek people. When villagers attempted to resist them, then Hector and his men punished them, not just by shooting them but by tearing out eyes and cutting mouths so that people died smiling. Hector explained to Mandras that the villagers were Fascists and loyal to the king, and that a good lesson would help them to change their ways.

Mandras also learnt to rape women and to enjoy their screams, since it was all in a good cause. A new and better Greece would be built, and you did what you liked with the inferior bricks that were going to be thrown away anyway. It was like making an omelette and throwing away the eggshells, said Hector, and Mandras drank in every word his leader said.

## Chapter 7   A Problem with Eyes

Pelagia treated the captain as badly as she could. If she served him food, she would deliberately spill it as she put it down, and eventually she noticed that he had acquired the habit of not pulling in his chair until she had already put the food on the table. His failure to protest at her treatment of him and his constant politeness made her even more annoyed. Her anger was so deep and so bitter that she needed to shout at him or even strike him in order to release it. After two months of sleepless nights, months during which she had done her best to annoy him, the captain remained calm and friendly.

One day he left his gun on the table. After some thought, Pelagia decided to put the gun in a bowl of water for a few minutes in the hope that this would do some damage. The captain came in and caught her just as she was lifting the gun out of the water. She heard a voice behind her and, in her fear, dropped it back in the bowl.

'Oh God,' she exclaimed, 'you frightened me!'

The captain looked down at the gun, raised his eyebrows

and said coolly, 'I see you're trying to make trouble for me.'

This was not what she had expected, but nevertheless her heart beat faster with fear and anxiety. 'I was washing it,' she said weakly at last. 'It was terribly oily.'

'How charming to know so little about guns,' said the captain. Pelagia went red, strangely angered by his suggestion, which she knew he did not mean, that she was a sweet and silly girl who did stupid things.

'You are not a good liar,' the captain added.

'What do you expect?' she demanded, immediately wondering what she had meant.

The captain seemed to know, however. 'It must be very difficult for you all to have to put up with us.' He removed the gun from the bowl, sighed and said, 'I suppose you have done me a favour. It does need cleaning.'

'Aren't you angry, then? Why aren't you angry?'

'What's anger got to do with music? Do you really believe I've got nothing important to think about? Let's just think about important things and leave one another in peace. I'll leave you alone and you can leave me alone.'

This idea struck Pelagia as new and unacceptable. She did not want to leave him alone, she wanted to shout at him and hit him. Suddenly overcome with emotion, she struck him with all her force, right across the left cheek. He tried to step back in time, but was too late. He steadied himself and touched a hand to his face, as if comforting himself, then held out the gun. 'Put it back in the water,' he said, 'I might find it less painful.' This remark made Pelagia even angrier. She rushed out into the yard and kicked an iron pot, injuring her toe, then threw the pot over the wall. The captain, watching her from the window, shook his head in amazement. These Greek girls, such passion and fire, he thought admiringly, and then wondered why no one had ever written an opera set in modern Greece. A tune entered his mind and he began to sing it softly to himself, thinking that perhaps he would call it 'Pelagia's March'.

As the months went by, Pelagia noticed that she was losing her anger, and this puzzled and upset her. The fact was that the captain had become as much a part of the house as the goat or her own father, and she was quite used to seeing him playing with little Lemoni in the yard, or seated at the table, deep in concentration, composing music for the mandolin. Early in the morning she looked forward with pleasure to the moment when he would enter the kitchen and say, '*Kalimera,** *Kyria* Pelagia. Is Carlo here yet?' and in the evening she would actually begin to worry if he were a little late.

A new source of anger developed, the problem being that this time the anger was directed against herself. It seemed that she just could not help looking at him, and he was always catching her. There was something about him, sitting at the table as he went through his paperwork, that made her look up at him regularly. But every time she looked up, he did too, and she would be caught in his steady gaze as surely as if he had grasped her by the wrists.

For a few seconds they would look at one another and then she would grow red and look down. Then a few seconds later she would look up, and at that moment he would return her glance. It was impossible and embarrassing. 'I've got to stop doing this,' she would tell herself and, certain that he was deep in his tasks, would look up and get caught again.

She knew he was playing a game with her, that she was being played with so gently that it was impossible to protest. After all, she had never caught him looking at her, so it was all her fault, obviously. Nevertheless, it was a game of which he was in absolute command, and in that sense she was its victim. She

* *kalimera*: Greek for *good morning*.

decided that she would not be the one to look down; she would wait until he broke away. She searched for every last bit of courage and looked up.

They looked at one another for what seemed like hours and Pelagia wondered foolishly if it was considered acceptable to blink. Her eyes began to water and she started seeing two captains instead of one. He did not look away but began to make funny faces, showing his teeth like a horse, and moving the tip of his nose from side to side, so that Pelagia began a smile, then laughed aloud and blinked. Corelli jumped to his feet, crying, 'I won! I won,' and the doctor looked up from his book, exclaiming, 'What? What?'

'You cheated,' protested Pelagia, laughing. The doctor looked from the captain to his daughter, adjusted his glasses and sighed. 'Whatever next?' he demanded, knowing perfectly well what was next, and working out in advance how to deal with it.

Some days later they passed each other at the door, she going out and he returning from work. Unselfconsciously, she raised one hand to his left cheek and, in passing, kissed him on the other. He was astonished and, by the time she reached the entrance to the yard, so was she, because it was not until then that she realized what she had done. She stopped as if she had walked straight into a wall, felt her blood rising to the roots of her hair, and realized that she did not dare look back at him. He called out, as she knew he would, '*Kyria* Pelagia.'

'What?' she demanded.

'What's for dinner?'

'Don't laugh at me. I thought you were my father. I always kiss him like that when he comes in.'

'Very understandable. We are both old and small.'

'If you are going to laugh at me, I shall never speak to you again.'

He came out and threw himself upon his knees before her.

38

'Oh no,' he cried, 'not that. Shoot me, beat me, but don't say you'll never speak to me.' He grasped her round the knees and pretended to weep.

'The whole village is looking,' she protested. 'Stop it at once.'

'My heart is broken,' he cried and, taking her hand, he began to cover it with kisses.

'Stupid goat, you are insane.'

Corelli laughed and got to his feet. 'Come inside,' he said, 'I've got something very interesting to show you.'

Relieved by this sudden change of subject, she followed him through the door, but found that he was passing her on the way out again. He put his hands on each side of her head, kissed her dramatically on the forehead, exclaimed, 'I'm sorry, I thought it was the doctor,' and then ran away across the yard and down the street. She stared after him in amazement, making every effort not to laugh or smile.


## Chapter 8    Snails

When the doctor glanced out of the window and saw Captain Corelli creeping up behind Lemoni in order to surprise her, he laid down his pen and went out into the afternoon sunlight.

'Excuse me, children,' said the doctor, ignoring the captain's embarrassment, 'Lemoni, do you remember that you told me you know a place where there were lots of snails? Can you come round this evening and show me where they are?'

Lemoni nodded importantly.

'What's all this about?' asked the captain.

Stiffly, the doctor said, 'Thanks to you Italians, there's almost no food. We're going out this evening to find snails.'

The captain wiped the sweat from his forehead and said, 'Permit me to come and help.'

So in the evening, an hour before sunset, Pelagia and her father, Lemoni and the captain climbed over a low wall and then began crawling through impossibly thick undergrowth in their search for snails. It became immediately apparent that there were quantities of snails everywhere they looked. The child and three adults became so involved in their task that they did not notice they had become separated. The captain found himself on his own and paused for a second, realizing that he could not remember ever having felt so content.

'Oh, oh no,' came Pelagia's voice from nearby.

Fearing that perhaps she had been hurt, the captain crawled towards the place where her voice had come from and found her unable to move, her hair caught in some briars, her neck pulled backwards. 'Don't laugh,' she said crossly.

'I'm not laughing,' he said, laughing. 'I was afraid you were hurt.'

'If you don't help me, I'll murder you. Just stop laughing.'

'Hold still,' he told her, and reaching over her shoulders he began to pull the hair out piece by piece, as gently as he could. 'I've done it,' he said, pleased with himself, and as he drew back and his lips passed her cheek, he kissed it tenderly, before the ear.

She touched her fingertips to the place of the kiss, and said, shaking her head at him, 'You shouldn't have done that.'

He knelt back and held her gaze with his own. 'I couldn't help it. I'm sorry.'

They looked at one another for a long moment, and then Pelagia began to cry. 'What's the matter?' asked Corelli, frowning in concern as Pelagia's tears rolled down her cheeks and fell into the bucket among the snails. 'You're drowning them,' he said, pointing. 'What's the matter?'

She gave a sad smile, and started crying again. He took her in his arms and patted her back. Suddenly she said, 'I can't stand it any more, not any of it. I'm sorry.'

'Everything is horrible,' agreed the captain, wondering if he too might start to cry. He took her head gently in his hands and touched at the tears with his lips. She gazed at him wonderingly and suddenly they found themselves underneath the briars, in the sunset, surrounded by escaping snails, deep in their first, secret, guilty kiss. Hungry and desperate, filled with light, they could not move away from each other, and when finally they returned home, they brought back fewer snails together than Lemoni brought on her own.

They became lovers in the old-fashioned sense. Their idea of making love was to kiss in the dark under the trees or sit on a rock watching the sea. He loved her too much to risk her unhappiness, and she had too much sense to take risks. Again and again she had seen the tragedy of girls with an unwanted child and the poisoned deaths of girls who had tried to end their pregnancies.

It was hard for Pelagia to love an invader and sometimes she shouted at Corelli, her eyes filled with tears of anger: 'How can you bear to be here? Orders? Orders from a madman! Don't you know you're being used? Why don't you take your guns and leave? Don't you know who the enemy is?'

At these times the captain listened silently and bowed his head, the bitterness of his shame eating like a worm at the muscles of his heart. But they could not stop themselves from loving one another.

Günter Weber managed to obtain a motorcycle for the captain, who turned up outside the doctor's house one day wearing a cap and goggles.

'Do you want to come for a ride?' he asked.

Pelagia crossed her arms. 'I've never been on one. In fact I've never been in a car either and I'm not starting now.'

'I've never been on one either,' he said, 'but it's very easy.'

'Somebody might see us,' said Pelagia.

The captain solved this problem by bringing Pelagia a disguise

41

consisting of a cap, goggles and a long leather coat, and the next day they met around the bend of the road and rode off on the bike. They fell off twice, without injury, and she gripped his waist, whitefaced with terror. She climbed off, shaking, and realized she could not wait to get back on; it was splendid to ride a motorcycle.

They went to places where Pelagia could not have been recognized and to places that were deserted, and there she would put her arm through his and walk beside him, leaning her weight against his shoulder, always laughing. With him, she would always remember that she laughed. One day they discovered a ruined hut so old that the floor had sunk into the earth. They called it 'Casa Nostra',* and in this secret house they would spread a blanket and lie embracing and talking.

All their lovers' talk began with the phrase, 'After the war'.

'After the war, when we are married, let's go to America; I've got relatives in Chicago. After the war we won't bring up our children with any religion, they can make their own minds up when they're older. After the war, we'll go all over Europe and you can give concerts in hotels and that's how we'll live. After the war I'll love you, I'll love you forever after the war.'

◆

It was during this period of happiness for Pelagia and the captain that Dr Iannis was woken one night by a gentle tapping on his window. Puzzled, the doctor looked out and saw a villager accompanied by a very tall fair-haired man wearing the Greek national costume, something that a wealthy man might wear once a year on a feast day. 'We thought you were the man to help him,' the villager told the doctor, before departing. The tall stranger smiled and held out his hand, speaking in an extraordinarily old-

---

* *Casa Nostra*: Italian for *our home*.

fashioned Greek that the doctor found almost impossible to understand. The stranger then climbed, uninvited, through the doctor's window into the house, and took a huge radio out of his bag. Pelagia woke and came into her father's room, saw the stranger and put her hand over her mouth, wide-eyed with amazement.

'Who's this?' she demanded of her father.

'How am I supposed to know,' replied the doctor. 'He says he's called Bunnios and he talks Greek like a Spanish cow.'

The stranger bowed politely and shook Pelagia's hand, then smiled charmingly and said, 'Greek of the old days. Homer.'*

'Ancient Greek?' exclaimed Pelagia, disbelievingly. The doctor tapped his finger to his forehead. 'English?' he asked.

'English,' agreed the man. 'But, I must beg you . . .'

'Of course we won't tell anyone.'

The man smiled. It had been an awful burden to speak the finest ancient Greek and not be understood.

'We are having an Italian officer sleeping in a room,' said the doctor, whose English was not as good as he liked to believe, 'so we are being very quiet, please. Are you a spy?'

The man nodded and asked, 'Do you have any clothes I could have? I would be so grateful.'

The Englishman departed for the town of Argostoli at dawn, wearing trousers that ended half way down his legs, and having received some good advice from the doctor: 'Look, OK? You accent terrible-terrible. Not to talk, understand? You are quiet until you learning. Also, you watch out Communists – they thieves. Italians OK, Germans not good, see?'

Bunnios, whose real name was Bunny Warren, soon found an empty hut in the hills where, using his huge radio, he reported in great detail to his British masters, informing them of troop

* Homer: an ancient Greek writer.

movements in the area. He also set himself the task of learning modern Greek, and was assisted in this by the willing islanders.

◆

The captain's opera group, La Scala, became accustomed to meeting in the doctor's house.

'Your soldiers are stealing from people's vegetable patches, when we're dying of hunger already,' said the doctor to Corelli one day, when the group was there.

'If it's true, they will be punished,' the captain replied, already deeply shamed and embarrassed by the fact that some nights previously someone, obviously an Italian soldier, had stolen Pelagia's goat.

'We Germans do not do this,' said Günter Weber, with a pleased expression on his face.

'Germans can't sing,' replied Corelli, 'and anyway, I'll get this investigated and I'll put a stop to it. It's too bad.'

Weber smiled. 'You are very famous for defending the rights of the Greeks. I wonder if sometimes you understand why you are here.'

'I try to think of it as a holiday. I don't have your advantages, Günter.'

'Advantages?'

'Yes. I don't have the advantage of thinking that other races are inferior to mine.'

'It's a question of science,' said Weber. 'You can't alter a scientific fact.'

Corelli frowned. 'Science? I don't care about science. Moral principles are important, not science.'

'We disagree,' said Weber in a friendly fashion. 'Science tells us that the strong survive. Strength needs no excuses and doesn't have to give reasons.'

'Science is about facts, and morality is about values,' said Carlo, who had been listening closely.

'It's also a matter of being able to live with yourself,' Corelli added.

'You're a good man,' said Günter, 'I admit it. Why don't I get my record player from my car and we can all sing with Marlene Dietrich.'* He went to his car and proudly returned with the record player, which he put down on the table. He put on the record and Dietrich began to sing, her voice full of the sadness of knowledge, the longing for love.

'Oh,' exclaimed Weber, 'her voice makes me melt,' and Corelli said, 'Antonia likes this. She's going to sing.' He began to accompany the song, playing so beautifully that in the village people stopped what they were doing and listened to Corelli fill the night. Pelagia left the kitchen, her form ghostlike in the light of the candles. 'Please play that song again,' she asked Weber. 'It was so beautiful.'

'Do you like it?' asked Weber, and she nodded. 'All right,' he continued, 'when I go home after the war, I'll leave it with you. It would please me very much for you to have it.'

Pelagia was delighted. She looked at the smiling boy with his smart uniform and blond hair and was filled with pleasure. 'You're so sweet,' she said, and kissed him naturally on the cheek, so that the boys of La Scala cheered and Weber went red and hid his eyes with his hand.

◆

The time came when the doctor decided that it was necessary to discuss certain matters with Pelagia. 'There's something I have to talk to you about,' he told her. 'It has not escaped my notice that you have fallen in love with the captain.'

* Marlene Dietrich: a famous film actress and singer, born in Germany.

She went violently red and looked terribly shocked. 'The captain?' she said foolishly.

He began a long speech. 'It's not that I don't like the captain. Of course, he's a little mad, which is quite simply explained by the fact that he is Italian. In fact I like him very much, but you must remember that you are engaged to Mandras, and technically, the captain is an enemy. Can you imagine the pain you will suffer when people discover that you have given up the love of a Greek in favour of an invader? People will throw stones at you and spit, you know that, don't you? You would have to move away to Italy if you wanted to stay with him, because here you might not be safe. Are you prepared to leave this island and this people?

'And another thing. Love is a temporary madness. When it ends you have to work out whether your roots have so joined together that it is unimaginable that you should ever separate. Because that is what love is. Love isn't breathlessness, it is not excitement, it is not lying awake at night imagining that he is kissing every part of your body. No, don't look so embarrassed, I'm telling you some truths. That is just being "in love", which any fool can do. Love itself is what is left over when being in love has burned away.

'I say to you that to marry the captain is impossible until our country is free again. I would be happy for you to do this, but this means that you have a love that will be delayed. Pelagia, you know as well as I do that love delayed means that physical passion increases. No, don't look at me like that. Do you think I don't know that young girls can be eaten by desire? Imagine if you got pregnant, what would you do? I would not assist in the murder of an innocent. Would you have the child, and then find that no man would ever marry you? I would not abandon you as long as I live, even under such circumstances. But imagine if I should die. What then?'

46

Pelagia had never felt so crushed in all her life and wept bitterly, but when she looked up, she found her father looking at her sympathetically. 'You make everything sound so disgusting,' she said. 'You don't know how it is.'

'I went through a lot of this with your mother,' he replied. 'She was engaged to someone else. I do know how it is.'

'You don't forbid everything then?' she asked hopefully.

'No, I don't forbid everything. I say you must be careful and act honourably to Mandras. Don't give in to your desires, that's all. The captain is a good man. Pray for our freedom, Pelagia, because then everything becomes possible.'

Pelagia stood up to go and her father said, 'I did not intend to upset you. I was young once.'

'Not everything was different in your day, then,' she said as she left the room, and her father smiled, pleased that his words had not crushed his daughter's spirit.

◆

The doctor and the captain were sitting indoors at the kitchen table while the latter was removing a broken string from his mandolin. The doctor leaned back and sighed, then suddenly asked, 'Are you and Pelagia planning to be married? As her father, I think I have a right to know.'

The captain was so surprised by the frankness of the question that he was unable to think of a reply. His relationship with Pelagia had only been able to proceed on the basis that no one ever brought the issue out into the open. He looked at the doctor anxiously.

'You can't live here,' said the doctor. He pointed to the mandolin. 'If you want to be a musician, this is the last place to be. And I don't think that Pelagia could live in Italy. She is a Greek. She would die like a flower without sunlight.'

'Ah,' said the captain, for the lack of any intelligent remark.

47

'It's true,' said the doctor. 'I know you have not thought about it. Italians always act without thinking. Anyway, Pelagia is a Greek, that's my point. So can it work?'

There was a silence between the two men. 'I love her,' said Corelli at last, as if this were the answer to the problem, which to him it was.

'I know that. You'd have to live here, that's all,' said the doctor. 'You might have to choose between loving her and becoming a musician.'

The doctor left the room, more for dramatic effect than for any other purpose, and then came back in. 'And another thing. This is a very ancient land and we've had nothing except murder for two thousand years. We've got so many places full of bitter ghosts that anyone who goes near them or lives in them becomes heartless or insane. I don't believe in God, captain, but I do believe in ghosts. And there will be many more deaths. It's only a question of time. So don't make any plans.'


## Chapter 9    Autumn 1943: Betrayal

The Allies★ invaded Sicily, Italy's southern island, and so they betrayed their most loyal and courageous friend, Greece, and did not come to its aid. The angry Greeks demanded to know why their country, which was occupied by the Italians, had been ignored, and received no answers. The Allies had abandoned Greece, the little nation that had given Europe its culture and its heart. To make matters worse, during this period the Greek Communists were committing unimaginably vicious acts, but for a long time the world did not believe it.

★ The Allies: countries, including Britain, the US, the Soviet Union and France, that fought against Germany, Italy and Japan in the Second World War.

On Cephallonia, the Italian soldiers listened to their radios and followed the course of Allied progress up Italy, their homeland, while the German soldiers were angered and disgusted by the Italian army's lack of resistance to the Allies. Corelli and his brother officers sensed ice in the air, and visits between the Germans and the Italians became less frequent. When Weber turned up at meetings of La Scala, he seemed quiet and distant.

'What happens,' Corelli asked Pelagia with a troubled look, 'when we have to surrender before the Germans do?'

'We'll get married.'

He shook his head sadly. 'It's going to be a complete mess. There's no chance of the British coming. They're going straight for Rome. No one will save us unless we save ourselves. We should attack the Germans on the island now, while there aren't many of them, but our generals don't do anything. They say we should trust the Germans.'

'Don't you trust them?'

'I'm not stupid.'

'Come inside,' she said, 'my father's out.'

'There's no point. My mind is just a blank that's filled with worry.'

Corelli came to the doctor's house less often, and day and night he trained his men, working them hard in the terrible August heat, so that the sweat ran down their faces and arms, and the sun burned the flesh of their shoulders. They did not complain. They knew that the captain was right to prepare them.

He himself stopped playing the mandolin; there was so little time for it that when he picked it up it felt foreign in his fingers in comparison with a gun. He went home to Pelagia on his motorbike at times when her father was likely to be out, and he brought her bread, honey, bottles of wine, a photograph signed on the back with the words 'After the War . . .' written on it in his elegant, foreign–looking handwriting, and he brought her his tired, grey face, and his saddened eyes.

'My poor darling,' she would say, her arms about his neck, 'don't worry, don't worry, don't worry,' and he would move back a little and say, '*Koritsimou,*★ let me just look at you.'

And then came the time when Carlo was listening to the radio, trying to find a signal. It was 8 September, and the evenings had become much cooler than they had been before. Carlo had recently been thinking about Francesco and about the horror of Albania, and now more than ever he knew that it had all been a waste, and that his time in Cephallonia had been a holiday from a war that was going to destroy his life once more, perhaps forever. He found a voice and turned up the volume: '. . . all aggressive acts by Italian Armed Forces against the forces of the British and the Americans will cease at once, everywhere.' The Italians had formally surrendered to the Allies.

Outside, the bells of the island began to ring; they rang all over the island in the towns of Argostoli, Lixouri, Soulari, Dorizata. On the radio there was a message from Eisenhower, the American president: '. . . All Italians who take steps to rid themselves of the German presence in their country will have the assistance and support of the Allies . . .'

Carlo ran out and found Corelli just arriving on his bike, a great cloud of blue smoke behind him. 'Antonio, Antonio, it's all over, and the Allies have promised to help us,' he cried. He threw his enormous arms around the man he loved and picked him up, dancing in a circle. 'Carlo, Carlo,' the captain cried, 'put me down. Don't get so excited. The Allies don't care about us. We're in Greece, remember. Carlo, you don't know your own strength. You half killed me.'

'They'll help us,' said Carlo, but Corelli shook his head. 'If we

★ *koritsimou*: Greek for *my little girl*.

50

don't act now, we're finished. We've got to get the Germans on the island to surrender to us.'

That night the Italian warships in the harbours of the island sailed for home, without informing anyone they were going, or taking with them a single Italian soldier. In a terrible act of cowardice, the warships withdrew their protection from the soldiers on the island, so that the German soldiers laughed and Corelli's men smelled betrayal. Corelli waited at the telephone for orders, and when none came he fell asleep in his chair.

Carlo, now realizing that Corelli's pessimistic predictions were probably correct, wrote his captain a long letter in which he declared his undying love for him and also his unselfish hope that Corelli would find true happiness with Pelagia. Strangely convinced that he was going to die soon, Carlo added this letter to his other writings and brought them to the doctor's house, with the request that his papers should be placed in the hiding-hole under the trapdoor and only opened and read in the event of his death.

Like Corelli, Günter Weber also slept from time to time in his chair, waiting for orders, desperately tired and with all his confidence gone. He missed his Italian friends, but worse than that, his country was losing and he no longer felt proud and full of strength. He felt inferior and so betrayed by his country's allies, the Italians, that if he had been a woman he would have wept. He tried to pray but the words turned bitter in his mouth.

Corelli stopped his motorcycle on his way back to camp and beneath the shade of a tree, by a ruined wall, he sat and thought about going back to Italy, about surviving, about Pelagia. The truth was that he had no home and that was why he never talked about it. Mussolini had forced his family to move to Libya, and there they had been attacked by rebels and had died, while he lay in hospital with a high fever.

Of all the relatives' houses where he had stayed, which one was

51

home? He had no family except his soldiers and his mandolin, and his heart was there in Greece. Had he suffered so much pain, so much loneliness, had he finally found a place to be, only to have it torn away? His memories of his parents were as thin and indefinite as those of a ghost, and for the first time he began to feel as if Pelagia already belonged to his past. He thought about dying and wondered how long Pelagia would weep, and what a shame it would be to spoil her lovely flesh with tears; it broke his heart to imagine it. He wanted to reach out from beyond the grave and comfort her, even though he was not yet dead.

He went to the doctor's house and asked them to look after his mandolin, and Pelagia wrapped it in a blanket and put it under the hole in the floor. They told him about Carlo's visit, and how he had left a thick pile of papers with them. The captain had not known that Carlo had ambitions to be a writer and was curious about the content of the big man's papers. He thought that Pelagia looked very thin and almost ill, and when she sadly stroked his cheek, he almost did not know how to prevent his tears.

◆

After Italy's surrender to the Allies, General Gandin, leader of the Italian troops on Cephallonia, suffered terrible indecision about the course of action he should take. He had two choices. Compared to the number of Italian soldiers on the island, there were many fewer German troops, and he could insist that the German soldiers laid down their arms and surrendered to the superior Italian forces. If the Germans rejected this, then the Italian troops could theoretically attack and overcome them. But Gandin knew that he would receive no support from the Allies, and moreover, that he would have neither air nor sea support from his own country. He knew that the Germans still had a large number of bomber planes based in mainland Greece, and the thought of those death machines screaming over the island as they dropped their bombs filled him with horror.

These thoughts led the General to the second option, which was to surrender to the Germans, on condition that the latter gave written guarantees of the safety of the Italian soldiers on the island. This would mean trusting the Germans not to break their promises and attack the Italians. It was this second route that Gandin was tempted to take. He was, in a strange way, a man of honour, and still considered the Germans to be his allies.

Unlike General Gandin, the Italian troops on Cephallonia knew exactly what should be done. They heard from the radio that the Germans, as they withdrew in Italy, were killing and looting along the way and they could see no reason why the Germans would not do the same in Cephallonia, given the chance. While Gandin delayed, unable to make up his mind, and his soldiers became almost crazy with anger and fear, the Germans quietly flew more arms and troops to the island.

Finally General Gandin came to a decision. Despite the universal demand of his men that the Germans should be forced to surrender, the General agreed with the German leaders on the island that the Italians should be allowed to keep their weapons and peacefully leave Cephallonia. There were no ships, however, to take the Italians away, a point which did not seem significant to Gandin. Some of the Italian troops, guessing what was likely to happen, became deeply depressed, while others, like Corelli, developed an iron determination and prepared their men to the last degree for the terrible battle that they were certain lay ahead of them.

When the German bomber planes arrived, early in the afternoon, tipping their wings, it was almost a relief to the waiting Italians. Now everything was clear; it was at last obvious that the Germans had betrayed them and that every Italian soldier would have to fight for his life. Günter Weber knew that he would have to turn his weapons on his friends. Corelli knew that his musician's fingers, so well accustomed to the arts of peace, must now tighten around a gun. General Gandin knew too late that he had made the wrong decision and that, as a result, his men were going to die. Pelagia knew that a war that had always been somewhere else would now settle upon her home and turn its stones to dust.

The German planes attacked Argostoli first because that was where most Italian troops were concentrated. Gandin made the foolish mistake of bringing his troops into the town in increasing numbers, and this made it easier for the Germans to isolate and cut them down. Houses were crushed by the bombs and soldiers and islanders died in large numbers. More and more German soldiers were flown in, and spread all over the island, killing as they went. Everyone knew that no ships or planes would come to aid an island of Cephallonia's insignificance. On a hillside, Bunny Warren sat by his radio and tried to persuade his superiors that they should provide the Italians with air and sea support, but without success.

◆

Dr Iannis and his daughter sat side by side at their kitchen table, unable to sleep, holding each others' hands. Pelagia was weeping. The doctor wanted to relight his pipe, but out of respect for his daughter's feelings he allowed his hands to stay in hers, and he repeated, *'Koritsimou,* I am sure he is all right.'

'But we haven't seen him for days,' she cried. 'I just know he's dead.'

'If he was dead someone would have told us, someone from La Scala. They were all nice boys, they would let us know.'

'Were?' she repeated. 'You think they're all dead? You think they're dead too, don't you?'

'Oh God,' the doctor sighed.

It was on the morning of 22 September that Captain Antonio Corelli, knowing that his leaders were planning to surrender to the Germans, having had no sleep for three days, climbed on his motorcycle and sped towards Pelagia's house. He threw himself into her arms, resting his burning eyes upon her shoulder, and told her, 'We are lost. The British have betrayed us.'

She begged him to stay, to hide in the house, in the hole in the floor, with his mandolin and Carlo's papers, but he took her face in his hands, kissed her without the tears that he was too tired to weep, and then rocked her in his arms, squeezing her so tightly that she thought that her bones would crack. He kissed her again and said, '*Koritsimou*, this is the last time I shall ever see you. There has been no honour in this war, but I have to be with my boys.' With his head hanging down, he told her, '*Koritsimou*, I am going to die. Remember me to your father. And I thank God I have lived long enough to love you.'

She watched him go as he drove away on his motorcycle, the dust cloud surrounding his head, then she went inside and sat at the kitchen table, terror gripping her heart.

## Chapter 10    The Order to Kill

Günter Weber stood before his superior officer and, his face hard with determination, said, 'Sir, I must request that you give this task to someone else. I cannot carry it out.'

His superior raised an eyebrow but somehow failed to feel any anger. The truth was that in this position he hoped that he would have done the same.

'Why not?' he asked.

'Sir, it is against international law to murder prisoners of war. It is also wrong. I must request to be excused.'

'They have betrayed us, their allies.'

'I realize that, but I am not a criminal, sir, and I do not wish to become one.'

The officer sighed. 'War is a dirty business, you know that. We all have to do terrible things. For example, I like you and I admire you for taking this position, but I must remind you that the punishment for refusing to obey an order is death. I don't state this as a threat but as a fact of life. You know this as well as I do.' He walked to the window and then turned. 'They're all going to be shot anyway. Why add your death to theirs? It would be a waste of a fine officer.'

Günter Weber swallowed hard and his lips trembled so that he found it hard to speak. At last he said, 'I request that my protest is recorded and put in my file, sir.'

'Your request is granted,' said the officer and left the room.

Weber leaned against the wall and lit a cigarette, but his hands shook so much that he immediately dropped it.

'Let's sing, boys,' said Antonio Corelli, looking round the inside of the truck where his men sat, watched by expressionless German soldiers. One of the Italians was already tearful, others were praying, their heads bowed down to their knees. Corelli felt strangely happy, as if he were drunk with tiredness and the absolute certainty of death. Why not smile in the face of death? 'Let's sing, boys,' he repeated, 'Carlo, sing.'

Carlo gazed at him with eyes full of endless sorrow, and began very softly to sing a song from an opera they all loved, *Madame Butterfly*, and soon others joined in, when they felt able to. The tune comforted them, and it was easier to sing than to think on death; it gave the heart something to do.

When the truck arrived, Günter Weber's knees began to shake. Almost before it had arrived, it seemed that he had known that life had called him to the killing of his friends. He had not expected them to arrive singing the tune that he and La Scala had sung together late at night at the doctor's house, nor had he expected them to jump so lightly from the truck. He ordered a German soldier to put his friends against the wall, lit another cigarette and turned away, but finally he turned again and approached the Italians. More than half of them were praying, kneeling in the soil, and others wept like children at a death. Antonio Corelli and Carlo Guercio were embracing. Weber reached for his packet of cigarettes and approached them.

'Cigarette?' he asked them, and Corelli took one, Carlo refusing. Corelli looked at Weber and said, 'Your hands are trembling and your legs.'

'Antonio, I am very sorry, I tried . . .'

Corelli sucked on his cigarette and said, 'I am sure you did, Günter, I know how it goes.'

Weber's face trembled with the effort of hiding his tears, and at last he said suddenly, 'Forgive me.'

Carlo made a sound of disgust in his throat and said, 'You will never be forgiven.' But Corelli put his hand up to silence his friend and said quietly, 'Günter, I forgive you. If I do not, who will?'

Weber held out his hand. 'Goodbye, Günter,' said Corelli, taking it. Allowing his hand to remain in his former friend's, he shook it briefly one final time and released it. He linked an arm through Carlo's, and smiled up at him. 'Come,' he said, 'we two have been companions in life. Let's go together to heaven.'

It was a beautiful day to die. A few soft clouds hid the top of Mount Aenos and nearby a goatbell rang. Corelli realized that his own legs were shaking and that he could do nothing to prevent it. He thought about Pelagia, with her dark eyes, her passionate nature, her black hair. He saw her clearly in his mind's eye: making a blanket that grew smaller every day; arm in arm with her father, returning from the sea; kissing Günter Weber on the cheek at the offer of the record player. Pelagia, whose form had been so sweetly rounded, now so pale and thin.

A Croatian soldier approached Weber, a man who, in Weber's opinion, had a dangerously violent nature. The Croatian said, 'Sir, more will be arriving. We can't delay.'

'Very well,' said Weber. He closed his eyes and prayed, a prayer without words to a God who did not care.

There was nothing formal about the killings, and the victims were not lined up against the wall or made to face forwards. Many of them were left on their knees, praying or weeping or begging for mercy. Some stood smoking as if at a party, and Carlo stood next to Corelli, glad to die at last and determined to die a soldier's death. Corelli put one hand in his pocket to steady the shaking of his leg, and deeply breathed the Cephallonian air that held Pelagia's breath.

The German boys heard the command to fire and fired in disbelief. Those of them whose eyes were open aimed wide or high, or aimed to avoid a death. The Croatian soldier shot to kill, firing rapidly and taking careful aim.

Weber's head spun. His former friends were leaping and dancing in the rain of bullets, were crying out, stumbling to their knees, arms waving, their mouths filled with blood. But what no one had seen, even Weber, was that at the order to fire, Carlo had stepped quickly sideways in front of Corelli, and had gripped the latter's wrists so tightly that he was unable to move. Corelli stared wonderingly into the middle of Carlo's back as great holes burst though from inside the latter's body, releasing fountains of blood.

Carlo stood unbroken as one bullet after another entered his chest like white-hot knives. He stood perfectly still and counted to thirty, looked up at the sky and then threw himself over backwards. Corelli lay beneath him, unable to move, so astonished by this extraordinary, saintly act of love that he did not hear the Croatian soldier's voice.

'Italians, it's all over. If any of you are living, stand up now and you will go free.'

58

He did not see the two or three stand up and see them fall again as the Croatian shot them down. Then he heard the single shots as Weber, drunk with horror, wandered among the dead, putting those still living out of their pain. Next to his head he saw Weber's boot and he saw Weber bend down and look directly into his eyes where he lay trapped beneath Carlo's great weight. He saw the shaking gun approach his face, he saw the ocean of sorrow in Weber's eyes, and then he saw the gun withdrawn, unfired. He tried to breathe more freely, and realized he was having difficulty, not only because of Carlo's weight but because the bullets that had passed through his friend had also struck himself.

◆

Corelli lay beneath his friend for hours, their blood mixing in the soil, in their uniforms, in their flesh. It was not until evening that Velisarios came across the heap of tragic bodies, and recognized the man as big as himself who had once reached a hand across the barrier of war and offered him a cigarette. He looked down into the vacant and staring eyes, reached down and tried to close them. He failed, and was struck by the horror of leaving such a brother to the wind and birds. He knelt down and with a huge effort he lifted Carlo from the ground, and, as he did so, he saw the mad captain who was staying at the doctor's, the one whose 'secret' love for Pelagia was known and discussed by everyone on the island. The man's eyes were not vacant and they blinked. The lips moved. 'Doctor,' said the dying man. 'Pelagia.'

The strong man put Carlo against the wall. Then he carefully picked the captain up, felt how light he was, and set off across the stony fields to save his life.

Nobody knows the exact number of the Italian dead that lay upon the earth of Cephallonia, but at least four thousand were murdered, possibly nine thousand. The evidence was lost in flame, because the Germans, displaying knowledge of their guilt, burnt the bodies, cutting down trees that were a thousand years old to make the fires. They changed flesh into smoke, they put one dead boy after another across their shoulders and tipped them into the flames, working until their legs weakened and the flames became too hot to approach.

One of the bodies that they burned was the body of General Gandin, who trusted his enemies and tried to save his men. Another who died at this time was Father Arsenios, the priest from Pelagia's village. He wandered among the bodies and the flames until he was so mad with grief that he began to beat the heads and shoulders of the German soldiers with a stick. At first the soldiers, who had murdered thousands, did not know what to do, but then an officer came up behind Arsenios and fired a single shot into the back of his neck, exploding his brains.

Men and women and the few Italian soldiers who had escaped approached the fires as closely as the heat permitted and began to pull away the bodies at the edge of the fires. All of them thought the same things: 'Is this what it will be like under the Germans? How many of these boys could there have been? How many of these boys did I know? Can I imagine how it is to die of bleeding, slowly?'

At dawn a thick, black cloud hung over the land and blocked out the sun, and the people returned to their houses and locked their doors.

## Chapter 11   An Operation

When the door was suddenly kicked open just as it was getting dark, Pelagia's first thought was that it was the Germans, since she knew that all the Italians were dead. Like everybody else she had heard the sounds of battle and seen truck after truck pass by, bearing either cheering German soldiers or the dead bodies of

Italians. At night she had gone out with her father, whose cheeks were trembling with tears of anger and pity, and looked for lives to save among those bodies abandoned in the fires.

It had left her speechless, not with fear or sorrow, but with emptiness.

When the door flew open she was frightened, but she had nevertheless, somehow been expecting it. Her gun was ready in her pocket. She stood up, her hand tightening around the gun, her face colourless, and saw Velisarios, breathing hard. He advanced to the table and gently placed his burden on it.

'Who is it?' asked Pelagia.

'He's alive,' said Velisarios. 'It's the mad captain.'

She bent down to look with eyes full of both horror and hope, but she did not recognize him; there were too many holes, too much blood. She wanted to touch him but withdrew her hand. Where does one touch a man like this? The body opened its eyes and the mouth smiled. '*Kalimera, koritsimou,*' it said, and she recognized the voice.

'It's the evening,' she said foolishly. '*Kalispera,*★ then,' he whispered and closed his eyes.

Pelagia looked up at Velisarios, her eyes wide and desperate, and said, 'Velisarios, you have never done a greater thing. I'm going to get my father. Stay with him.' She found her father at the *kapheneion* and dragged him out, ignoring the angry stares of the other men, and Kokolios, who roared at her.

The doctor looked at the body and knew he had never seen anything worse. There was enough blood to fill the veins of a horse. 'It would be kinder to kill him,' he said, but before Velisarios could say, 'I thought so too,' Pelagia began beating her father with both hands. And so water was put on to boil and the rags of the captain's uniform were gently cut away.

★ *kalispera*: Greek for *Good evening*.

Dr Iannis complained as he cleaned away the blood. 'What am I supposed to do? I have no equipment to perform an operation.'

'Shut up, shut up, shut up,' Pelagia shouted, her heart racing with both fear and determination. 'Just shut up and do it.'

Because the doctor was unaware that most of the blood and flesh had belonged to the broad back of Carlo Guercio, it seemed unbelievable to him that Antonio Corelli was as little wounded as he was. Once he was cleaned, it was clear that the victim had six bullets in his chest, one in the stomach, and one through the outer flesh in his right arm. But the doctor knew too much to be optimistic and it still seemed hopeless. Frightened of the task that lay ahead of him, he opened a bottle of *raki*,* drank deeply and passed the bottle to Velisarios, who did the same. Then, with the comforting taste of alcohol in his mouth, he reached for an instrument and moved it gently around in each wound until he felt it reach a bullet.

He stood up amazed, realizing that the holes were not even deep and that the bullets should have passed right through the victim's body but had not done so. 'Daughter,' he said, 'I swear by all the saints that this man's flesh is made of steel. I think he'll live.'

'Antonio,' he called, and Corelli opened his eyes. 'Antonio, I'm going to operate. I haven't got much morphia. Can you drink?' Corelli nodded, and Pelagia poured a cup of *raki* down his throat while the doctor injected morphia into his arm. Pelagia looked at that desperately damaged body, helpless as a worm, and knew that it was not exactly a body that one loved, but that one loved the man who shone out through the eyes and used his mouth to smile and speak. The doctor saw her dreaming and said, 'Don't just sit there. We need more boiling water. And wash your hands, especially under the nails.'

* *raki*: very strong Greek alcohol.

Pelagia discovered in that hour how difficult the task was that she had set her father. Her hands trembled, and at first she could hardly force herself to touch the captain. She looked up and saw her father cutting wide holes around the bullet wounds and had to resist her desire to be sick. The doctor started on the bullet in the stomach, since he needed to do something that was relatively easy in order to increase his confidence. He found it not far beneath the surface of the skin and picked it out, amazed by its flattened shape. 'It's unbelievable,' he said, showing it to Pelagia. 'How do you explain this?'

'He was behind that big man, the one as big as me,' said Velisarios. 'The big man was holding him from behind, like this.' He stood up and put his hands behind his back to show how one could grip another's wrists. 'I think he was trying to save the man,' he said.

'Carlo,' said Pelagia, suddenly bursting into tears. Carlo was the first of the boys of La Scala whom they now knew with certainty was dead.

'No man who dies like that has died for nothing,' said the doctor, fighting back his own need for tears. Pelagia wiped her eyes on the sleeve of her dress and said, 'Antonio always said that Carlo was the bravest in the Army.'

'Velisarios, is the man's body still there? We would like to bury it and not see it burned,' said the doctor.

'It's after dark, I'll go and look,' said the strongman. 'On the way, I might kill a German, who knows?' He departed, happy to be out of that house where the sights were enough to make one ill.

When the doctor had finished cleaning out the wound, he gave Pelagia the task of sewing it up, and she did so with accuracy and care, despite her feeling of the unreality of it all. Velisarios buried Carlo Guercio's remains that night in the yard of the doctor's house. Just before dawn, when the operation on the captain was finished at last, and father and daughter were both utterly exhausted, they came out to say their goodbye to that heroic soldier.

Pelagia combed the hair and kissed the forehead, and Velisarios placed a cigarette in the dead man's lips. 'I owed him one,' he said. The doctor made a speech while Pelagia wept beside him. 'Sleep long and well,' he ended. 'As long as we remember you, you will be remembered fair and young.'

Leaning upon each other, the doctor and his daughter returned inside. Carefully, they carried Corelli to Pelagia's bed, and outside the first birds sang.

♦

It was only a short time before the Germans began to take an interest in loot. Not only did the doctor have to hide his valuables, he also had to hide an Italian officer who lay, unable to move, in his daughter's bed. Pelagia made a bed for him at the bottom of the hole in the kitchen, and once again Velisarios was called in to carry him. There Corelli was reunited with his mandolin and Carlo's papers were temporarily removed. The lid of the hiding-place was left open unless troops were in the neighbourhood.

For the first day after the operation the captain slept, but when he first woke, the pain was so bad that he could not move at all, and he felt as if he had been run over by a lorry.

'I can't breathe,' he told the doctor.

'If you couldn't breathe you couldn't speak.' The captain said nothing and the doctor continued, 'It appears that Carlo saved your life.'

'It doesn't "appear". I know he did. Of all of us, he died the best. And he's left me to remember it.'

'You shouldn't weep, Captain. We are going to get you well, and then get you off the island.'

'When I am better you must move me from the house, Doctor. I don't want you in danger. If am caught, I should die alone.'

'We can move you to your secret house, where you used to go with Pelagia. Don't look so surprised. Everybody knew. And you may not get better. Remember that.'

'My God, Doctor, please tell me some lies.'

'The truth will make us free. We overcome fear by looking it in the eyes.'

The captain fell into a fever two days later and Pelagia remained in the hiding-place with him, wiping his forehead to reduce his temperature. The fever came to a crisis on the fourth day, and Corelli was sweating so much and talking so nonsensically that both the doctor and Pelagia feared for his life. But two days later the fever left, and the patient opened his eyes with wonder, as if realizing that he existed for the first time. He felt weaker than it ought to be possible to feel, but by the same evening he was able to stand with the doctor's help and let himself be washed. Pelagia fetched a mirror and showed him his new-grown beard, and that night he was fed his first solid meal. Snails.

◆

In later life, Pelagia remembered the time of Corelli's recovery and his escape not as a period of exciting adventure, nor even as a time of fear and hope, but as the slow beginning of her sorrows. The war had reduced her anyway. Her skin, stretched tightly over her bones, was transparent from lack of food, and when she ate she chewed carefully in case she lost a tooth. Her rich black hair had thinned and lost its shine, and showed the first grey hairs that should not have appeared for at least another decade. It was hard to obtain food, and the doctor was reduced to trapping snakes and other such creatures. Things were not hopeless, however; there was always the sea, the source of Cephallonia's being.

65

As soon as Corelli could walk, he went in the company of the doctor and Velisarios to Casa Nostra at night, while Pelagia remained at home in the hiding-place in which the mandolin, the doctor's History and Carlo's papers had been replaced. As long as the German rapists were on the island, she hardly left the house. Corelli had given her his ring, too big for any of her fingers, and she turned it round and round in the lamplight. The captain came frequently, after dark, complaining that the hut was cold, his new beard scratching her cheeks as they lay fully clothed upon her bed, wrapped in each other's embrace, talking of the future and the past.

'I will always hate the Germans,' she said.

'Günter saved my life.'

'He murdered all your friends.'

'He had no choice. It wouldn't surprise me if he shot himself afterwards. He was trying not to cry.'

'There is always a choice.'

'He wasn't brave like Carlo. Only one in a million is made like that, you mustn't blame poor Günter.'

Pelagia desperately wanted to keep her captain on the island, but knew that she would kill him if she did. There were people who were prepared to betray for bread, and it could only be a matter of time before the Germans became aware of his presence in their lives. She asked Kokolios and Stamatis to enquire for news of Bunnios, the English spy, and to tell him to call on her if he could.

For some time now Bunny Warren had been encouraging the owners of boats to help the few surviving Italian soldiers to escape from the island, and it was easy for him to arrange the captain's departure. He called at Pelagia's home one night, tapping softly on her window, and when she had removed herself from Corelli's embrace, she looked out and saw the man whose help she had both sought and feared. He came in through the door and very formally shook her hand.

'Who is this?' asked Corelli, who for a moment had been fearing a visit from the Germans.

'Bunnios,' said Pelagia, without answering his question, 'this is an Italian soldier and we have to get him out.' By chance a boat was leaving for Sicily the following morning and it would be easy to put the captain on board. They simply had to go to a certain bay at one o'clock in the morning with a lamp, and flash out to sea in answer to the signals flashed from the boat.

Corelli did not go back to Casa Nostra before dawn, but stayed with Pelagia in the house. The three of them sat in that familiar kitchen, saddened and fearful, talking quietly and shaking their heads over all the memories.

'I owe my life to you, Doctor,' the captain said.

'I am sorry about the scars. It was the best I could do.'

'And I am sorry, Doctor, about the rape of the island. I don't suppose we will ever be forgiven.'

'As you know, Captain, I must have forgiven you, or I would not have given you permission to marry my daughter.'

Pelagia and Corelli looked at each other and the captain said, 'We have decided that if we have a son, we will name him Iannis.'

The doctor was visibly delighted, even though this was exactly what he would have expected under the circumstances. He looked up, his eyes watering, and said simply, 'Antonio, if I have ever had a son it was you. You have a place at this table.'

Corelli stood up and the two men embraced, clapping each other on the back, and then the doctor embraced his daughter. 'I'll leave you two children together,' he said. 'There is a little girl dying and I should visit.'

The doctor left the house and the two lovers sat opposite each other, unable to speak. Finally the tears began to follow each other slowly down Pelagia's cheeks, and Corelli knelt beside her, put his arms around her and laid his head against her chest. He was shocked again at how thin she was and closed his eyes tightly, imagining that it was another world. 'I am so afraid,' she said. 'I think you won't come back, and the war goes on and on forever, and there's no safety and no hope and I'll be left with nothing.'

'I shall not forget you and I will come back,' replied Corelli.

'Promise?'

'I promise. I have left you my ring and Antonia.'

'We never read Carlo's papers.'

'Too painful. We'll read them when I return.'

She stroked his hair in silence and said finally, 'Antonio, I wish that we had . . . lain together. As a man and woman.'

'Everything at the right time, *koritsimou*.'

'There may not be a time.'

'There will be. You have my promise.'

At eleven o'clock Bunny Warren scratched at the window. He carried a knife in his belt and sounded extremely efficient as he gave detailed instructions to the doctor, who translated them for Corelli's benefit.

It was a cold December night, there was no moon, and since most Germans preferred to be indoors on such a night, the journey to the beach was relatively safe. Nevertheless, Pelagia's heart beat fast and a dark hole seemed to be opening in her heart. Corelli felt so sad he almost wished that they would meet some German soldiers so that he could die, fighting and killing, and end it all. He knew that to leave the island would be to lose his roots.

For warmth, the four of them stood close together on the tiny patch of sand, waiting for the flash of a lamp that would come to them from the sea. Corelli walked to the waterline and, seeing the black waves, wondered how he would ever survive the journey. He felt his love for the island turning in his chest like the twist of a knife, because he had his own village now and even his thought and speech had changed. Returning to Pelagia, he held her face in his hands and then embraced her.

When the light flashed three times from the sea and Warren returned the signal, Corelli shook his hand, kissed his father-in-law on both cheeks and went to Pelagia once more. There was nothing to be said. He knew that her mouth was trembling with grief and his throat was tight with the same emotion. He stroked her cheek tenderly and kissed her eyes. He heard the sound of the boat approaching and looked up to see the shadows of two men inside it. The four approached the boat and the doctor said, 'Go well, Antonio, and return.'

'May God hear you,' said the captain, and for the last time he held Pelagia.

After he had climbed into the boat, disappearing into the darkness like a ghost, Pelagia ran into the waves until the sea reached her thighs, but though she tried to catch sight of him, she saw nothing. A terrible emptiness seized her and she put her hands to her face and wept, bent over in pain, her cries carried off in the wind and were lost in the sound of the sea.

## Chapter 12   1943–9: The Years of Terror

Of the German occupation there is little to say, except that it caused the islanders to feel more appreciation for the Italians they had lost. It seldom happens that a people can learn to feel friendly towards their oppressors, but hardly since Roman times had there been any other kind of rule in Cephallonia. Now there were no more Italians working in the fields beside the farmers in order to escape the boredom of army life, there were no more football matches between teams that quarrelled and cheated, there were no flirtations with girls by soldiers who had a cigarette hanging from the corners of their mouths. There were no more voices sending out opera tunes across the pine trees of the mountains. Gone were the charming chicken-thieves, and in their place came a period of time that the doctor recorded in his History as the worst time of all.

The islanders remember that the Germans were not human beings. They were machines without principles, machines that only knew how to loot and kill, without any passion except the love of strength, and without belief except in their natural right to destroy an inferior race.

The Italians had of course been thieves, but their shame when caught showed that they recognized their guilt. The Germans came into the house at any time of day, kicked over the furniture, beat the occupants, however old or young, and in front of their eyes carried away whatever they liked. Both Pelagia and her father were beaten at different times for no apparent cause. Drosoula had cigarettes burned into her skin for frowning at an officer. The doctor had all his precious medical equipment, gathered together over twenty years of poverty, broken in his presence by four officers whose hearts were as dark and empty as the caves of hell.

When in November 1944 the German troops were ordered to withdraw, they destroyed every building for which they found the time, and the inhabitants of Cephallonia rose up against them and fought them all the way to the sea.

But the night before he left, Günter Weber, who had ashamedly stayed away from the house since the time of the killings, brought his record player and his collection of Marlene Dietrich records and left them outside Pelagia's door, as he had promised in happier days. He wrote a note in Italian: 'God be with you, I will remember you always.'

Pelagia hid the record player in the hole in the floor, with Antonio's mandolin and Carlo's papers, and it survived the terrible years that followed.

◆

The Germans left and the celebrations began, but no sooner had the bells begun ringing than the members of the Communist organization ELAS, now calling themselves EAM, came out from hiding and attempted to take control of the country. They formed Workers' Councils and elected themselves to every post of authority. In Cephallonia the Communists began to send awkward characters to prison camps. On the mainland they poisoned, with dead animals, the water of villages that opposed them. Into mass graves they threw the dead bodies of Greeks who had had their eyes torn out and their mouths cut into the shape of a smile. They kidnapped 30,000 little children and sent them across the border into Communist Yugoslavia to be taught how to be true Communists. ELAS soldiers captured by the British were so frightened of their leaders that they begged to be allowed to remain in British prison camps.

Pelagia and the doctor were two out of millions of people whose lives were forever destroyed by these butchers. The doctor was dragged away in the night by three men who had decided that since he was a doctor he must be a Fascist. They threw Pelagia into a corner and beat her unconscious with a chair. When Kokolios came out from his house to defend the doctor, he too was carried away, even though he was a Communist. He was accompanied by Stamatis, a supporter of the royal family, and the three men were taken to the harbour for transportation.

Pelagia did not know what had happened to her father, and none of the authorities would tell her. Alone in the house, penniless and helpless, for the first time in her life she thought of ending everything by killing herself. The island seemed to be cursed by an endless series of oppressors. When would Antonio return? The war was continuing in Europe, and probably he was dead. She heard that the Communists had been killing the Italian soldiers who had come to fight alongside them against the Greeks. Had the time come, finally, to hate the Greeks? Of the

71

nations who had broken into her house to beat her and steal her possessions, only the Italians were innocent, it seemed.

Fortunately she had a friend. Drosoula had long known that Pelagia had lost her love for Mandras, and that by his long silence he had given up his rights. She knew also that Pelagia was waiting for an Italian, but she felt no bitterness and never uttered a single word of blame. When Pelagia stumbled bleeding through her door after the Communists had taken Dr Iannis, Drosoula, who had also suffered much, stroked her hair and uttered loving words, as if Pelagia were her own daughter. Within a week she had closed up her little house on the harbour and moved into the doctor's house on the hill. She found his Italian gun in a drawer and kept it at her side in case of attack.

Like Pelagia, Drosoula had been reduced by the war. The layers of fat had melted from her waist and thighs, and her great ugly moon of a face had sunk inwards. However, her tall, thin form and grey hairs demanded respect, and her unbroken spirit gave Pelagia strength.

For comfort they slept together in the doctor's bed, and by day they made plans to find supplies of food and listened to each other's complaints and stories. They dug for roots in the undergrowth, and Drosoula took her young friend down to the harbour to learn to fish.

But Drosoula was out when Mandras returned, full of self-importance and new ideas, expecting the admiring attention of the young woman he had not seen for years, and determined to take revenge. He came in through the door without knocking and leaned his gun against the wall. When she heard the noise in the kitchen, Pelagia, who was in her room, called out, 'Drosoula?' A man came in who she did not recognize, except that he looked very like Drosoula had done before the war; there was the same swollen stomach and thighs, the same round, coarse face and thickened lips. Puzzled, Pelagia stood up.

Mandras also was confused. There was something about this desperately thin, frightened girl that reminded him of Pelagia, but this woman had silver threads in her thin black hair, her blouse and skirt hung straight to the ground, her cheeks were hollow. He looked quickly around the room to see whether Pelagia was there, assuming that this must be a cousin or an aunt. 'Mandras, is it you?' said the woman, and he recognized the voice.

He stood, amazed and confused, with much of his hatred knocked out of him, while she looked at those coarse and altered features and felt deep disgust. 'I thought you must be dead,' she said finally.

He closed the door and leaned against it. 'You mean you were hoping I was dead. As you see, I am not. I am very much alive and well. Don't I get a kiss from my fiancée?'

She advanced fearfully and placed a kiss on his right cheek.

'I am glad you are alive,' she said.

He caught both her wrists and held them tightly. 'I don't think you are. How is your father, by the way? Is he not here?'

'Let me go,' she said softly, and he did so. 'The Communists took him away,' she told him.

'Well, he must have done something to deserve it.'

'He did nothing. He healed the sick. And they beat me with a chair and took everything.'

'There must be reasons. The party is never wrong. Whoever is not with us is against us.'

She noticed that he wore the red star of ELAS sewn into the front of his cap. 'You're one of them,' she said.

He leaned against the door, placing all his weight against it, increasing her sense of imprisonment and her fear. 'Not just one of them, an important one of them,' he stated, sounding pleased with himself, then added challengingly, 'Soon we will have a nice big house to live in. When shall we get married?'

She trembled and, seeing this, his anger increased. 'We will not be married,' she said. 'We were very young, it was not what we thought it was.'

'Not what we thought? And there was I, fighting for Greece, thinking of you all day and dreaming of you at night. And now I come back at last and find a faded cow who has forgotten me.'

'What's the matter with you?' she asked.

'The matter with me?' He took from his pocket a thick bundle of papers. 'This is what is the matter with me.' He threw them towards her feet and she picked them up slowly. She held the bundle in her hands and realized that it consisted of her letters to him in Albania. 'My letters?' she said, turning them over in her hands.

Mandras gave a sudden roar of disgust and, seizing the letters, he found the last one, held it up to the light and read, 'You never write to me, and at first I was sad and worried. Now I realize that you cannot care and this has caused me to lose my love for you also. I want you to know that I have decided to release you from your promises. I am sorry.'

He gave a smile that was both humourless and threatening. 'Yes, I'm able to read now, and this is what I found in the letters I had been carrying next to my heart. And now I know the truth. Do you know the first thing I heard when I arrived back here? I heard, "Mandras, did you hear about your old fiancée? She's going to marry an Italian." So you've found a Fascist for yourself, have you? Is this what I've been fighting for, you cow?'

Pelagia stood up, her lips trembling, and said, 'Mandras, let me out.'

'Let me out,' he repeated, 'let me out. Poor little thing's frightened, is she?' He came up to her and struck her across the face so hard that she spun round before she fell. He kicked her in the stomach and bent down to pick her up by the wrists, then he threw her on the bed and, quite against his original intentions, began to tear at her clothes.

74

This rape of women was something that he could not help, it seemed. It was a feeling that came from deep inside him, something he had learned in years of not needing to explain his actions to anyone. It was his natural right, and the violence was much more exciting than the sexual act itself.

But Pelagia fought. Her nails broke in his flesh, she struck him with hands and knees and elbows, she screamed and struggled. To Mandras her resistance was unreasonable, he was failing despite his weight and strength, and he sat back and hit her repeatedly. Then suddenly he tried to pull up her skirts. The solid weight of her gun fell out of its pocket and landed beside her head on the pillow, but Mandras did not see it, and when the bullet cracked through his shoulder, the shock knocked him backwards and he gazed at Pelagia in shock and accusation.

Drosoula heard the crack of the gunshot just as she came through the kitchen door and at first she did not recognize the sound, but then she knew what it was and took the Italian gun from the drawer. Without thinking, knowing that thought would make her a coward, she pushed open the door of Pelagia's room and saw there the unthinkable.

She had thought that Pelagia might have shot herself, that there might be thieves, but when she burst in, she saw the doctor's daughter leaning up on her elbow, her face swollen and bloody, her lips split, her clothes torn. Drosoula followed Pelagia's gaze and saw, leaning against the wall behind the door, a man who might have been her son. She ran to Pelagia's side and took her into her arms, rocking her, and heard the words, 'He . . . tried . . . to . . . rape me.'

Drosoula stood up, and mother and son examined each other in disbelief. So much had changed. As the anger grew in the woman, the fire in Mandras died. A wave of self-pity overcame him and all he wanted to do was weep; everything had come to nothing, everything was lost. The horror of the war in Albania, the years in the forest, his new power and importance, it was all a dream, and he was a frightened little boy again, trembling before the anger of his mother. And his shoulder hurt so much. He wanted to show it to her, to win her attention. He wanted her to touch and heal it.

But she pointed the gun at him and spat the one word that seemed to mean the most, 'Fascist'.

'Mother . . .' he said in a voice that was low and frightened.

'How dare you call me "mother"? I am no mother and you are not my son. I have a daughter . . .' she pointed to Pelagia, who had curled into a ball, '. . . and this is what you do. I do not know you, never in my life do I want to see you again, I have forgotten you, my curse goes with you. May you never know peace, may your heart burst in your chest, may you die alone.' She spat on the ground and shook her head with disgust. 'Pig rapist, get out before I kill you.'

Mandras left his gun leaning against the wall of the kitchen, and with bright red blood on his right hand where he still held his wound, he stumbled out into the cold December sun. He looked through tearful eyes at the tree where once he had swung and laughed, and where, he seemed to remember, there had once been a goat. It was a tree that was incomplete without Pelagia as she was, fresh and beautiful, slicing onions beneath it and smiling through the tears. A wave of grief overcame him and his throat tightened with sorrow.

It did not occur to him that he was just one more life twisted and ruined by the war. He was aware only that heaven had disappeared, that hope had turned to dust, that joy, which had once shone brighter than the summer sun, had disappeared into the black light and cold heat of mass murder. He had struggled for a better world and instead had destroyed it.

There was once a place where all had shone with delight and innocence. He stood still for a moment, recalling where it was;

then he went down to the sea, stood on the waterline, and kicked off his boots. With his right hand he slowly removed his clothes till he stood with nothing on. He realized he wanted only to feel the sea and sand upon his skin. He needed to be washed.

He remembered days in his boat with nothing to do except fish; he remembered his joy when something fine was landed for Pelagia, his pleasure at her pleasure when he gave it to her. He remembered that in those days he was beautiful. He began walking into the sea that would take his life, and by drowning him make him clean, make him pure and innocent once more.

## Chapter 13    Antonia

There had been so many rapes that Pelagia and Drosoula were not surprised to find an abandoned bundle on their doorstep. It had been born at a time when its father could have been a German or a Communist, and the mother might have been any unfortunate girl at all. Whoever this sorrowing and dishonoured girl had been, she had cared enough about her child to leave it upon the doorstep of a doctor's house, knowing that those inside would be able to cope. The disorder of the times was so great that the two women could think of no solution except to try and care for it themselves, thinking that in time the child could be adopted by someone childless or handed to a charitable organization.

They had taken the child inside and unwrapped it and discovered that it was a girl. She was very calm and cried only a little. She sucked the thumb of her right hand (a habit she never lost, even in old age), and she smiled a lot, her legs and arms waving up and down in delight.

The two women, who had suffered so greatly from loss and unhappiness, found that the child, whom they named Antonia, gave new meaning to their lives. Because of her, the women's tragic memories began to fade, and she took her place in their lives as if she had always been meant to be there. In all her life, Antonia never asked a question about her father, and only when she applied for a passport to go abroad did she discover that she did not officially exist.

She did have a grandfather, however. When Dr Iannis returned after two years, stumbling into the kitchen supported by two charity workers, utterly broken by his treatment in the prison camp and forever speechless, he bent down and kissed the child before retiring to his room. Just as Antonia did not enquire about a father, Dr Iannis did not enquire about the child. It was enough for him to know that the world had gone down a path that he had no hope of understanding. He accepted that his daughter and Drosoula would sleep in his bed, and that he would take Pelagia's, because, whichever bed it was, he would dream the same dreams of a forced march of hundreds of kilometres without his boots, without food or water. He would hear the cries of villagers as their houses burned, the crack of gunshots as they were murdered, and he would witness, over and over again, Stamatis and Kokolios dying in each other's arms and begging him to leave them in the road in case he himself was shot.

In his wordlessness, Dr Iannis drew the same comfort from Antonia that he had drawn from his daughter after his own young wife had died. He would put the child upon his knee, arranging her black hair, gazing into her brown eyes as if this alone was the way to speak, her smile filling his heart with sorrow, because when she was old she would lose her innocence, and learn that tragedy destroys the muscles of the face until a smile becomes impossible.

In 1949 the national government succeeded at last in defeating the Communists, who lost their control of the country. Dr Iannis took up medicine again, helping his daughter in a reversal of their roles. It upset Pelagia to see the shaking of his hands as he dealt with patients' wounds, and she knew also that he worked despite a terrible sense of uselessness. Why preserve life when all of us must die, when health is only an accident of youth? She wondered sometimes at the strength of his desire to heal, despite all he had suffered. In the evening she wrapped her arms around him and held him as his mind wandered back over the past, his eyes wet with sadness, and she buried her head on his chest, understanding that by comforting him she was comforting herself too.

She attempted to interest him in working on his History, and when she took the papers from the hiding-hole and arranged them in front of him at his table, he seemed willing enough to work. He read through them, but at the end of a week Pelagia found he had added only one short paragraph in a shaky handwriting that did not look like his old, firm handwriting at all. Then she saw that across the bottom of the last page her father had written, 'In the past the horrors came from outside. Now we have only ourselves to blame.'

While she had been in the hiding-hole, Pelagia had rediscovered Antonio's mandolin and Carlo's papers. She read through the latter in a single evening and was astonished; she had never imagined that that powerful, good-natured man had suffered so greatly from a secret sadness that had made him a stranger to himself. She saw that he had been as determined to lose his life as he had been to save Corelli's and she realized that if her own adopted child was at risk, she would find the same extraordinary courage in herself.

Antonia grew tall and lovely, a child whose movements were filled with confidence and grace. She was incapable of behaving like a 'lady', and when she sat in her grandfather's armchair she not only sucked her thumb but also hung one leg over the arm of the chair, ignoring her mother's and Drosoula's protests with laughing cries of, 'Don't be so old-fashioned.'

The family were regarded as eccentric. The empty-headed gossips of the village regarded Drosoula, with her extreme ugliness, and Pelagia, with her assumption that she was any man's equal, as a pair of crazy women. Children threw stones at them as they passed, and adults warned their children to keep away and encouraged their dogs to bite them. Nevertheless, Pelagia earned a living, because after darkness people would arrive secretly in the belief that her treatments were sure to work.

During all this time Pelagia became certain that Antonio Corelli was dead and, like her father, she also became certain beyond doubt of the reality of ghosts.

It had happened first in 1946 when, one day in October, she was standing outside the house with the infant Antonia in her arms. She was making baby noises and giving the baby her finger to suck, when something made her look up. She saw a figure dressed in black, standing before her in exactly the same place that Mandras had been when he had been shot by Velisarios' cannon. The figure was looking at her, as if it wanted to take a step towards her, and her heart leapt. There was an atmosphere around him of nine thousand weeping ghosts, and sorrow seemed to pour from his face. Thin and bearded though he was, she was sure it was him. Excited beyond all joy, she put the baby down in order to run to him, but when she looked up he had gone.

Her heart jumping in her chest, she ran. Around the bend she stopped and looked wildly around, crying out, 'Antonio! Antonio!' But no voice responded and no man came towards her. He had disappeared. Her hands rose to the sky in confusion and fell down again to her sides. She stood watching and calling until her shouts hurt her throat and tears blinded her eyes.

The same ghost appeared at the same place in 1947 and every year after that at roughly the same time, but never exactly. It was because of this that Pelagia came to the conclusion that Antonio had kept his promise to return and that it was possible to keep such a promise and continue to love even from beyond the grave. She was able to live satisfied, knowing that she had not been abandoned, and, filled with happy dreams of being desired and loved, she looked forward to her own death when she would once again have all that had been stolen away in life.

## Chapter 14    1953: Earthquake

The thirteenth of August, 1953 was a fine day, with small white clouds scattered here and there most charmingly in the deep blue sky. That morning Antonia, now eight years old but as tall as a child of twelve, went to pick up a sheet of paper from the floor, and when the sheet flew upwards and stuck to her hand, she cried, 'It's magic,' and ran excitedly outside.

Strange things were happening all over the Ionian islands. There were no birds in the sky; on the hillsides and in the undergrowth, snakes and rats left their holes, and in the villages all the dogs began barking.

Drosoula came inside sweating and shaking and told Pelagia, 'I am ill, I feel terrible, something has happened to my heart.' She sat down heavily with her hand to her chest, taking deep breaths, and Pelagia went to her medicine cupboard and made a drink for her. Antonia, who had come back inside, suddenly burst into tears, exclaimed, 'Mama, I've got to get out,' and ran outdoors.

Drosoula and Pelagia were exchanging surprised glances when suddenly there came a low, terrible roar from the earth that made the two women feel as if their hearts were exploding in their chests. 'A heart attack,' thought Pelagia desperately, and she saw Drosoula, with her hands on her stomach and her eyes staring, stumble as if someone had struck her.

It seemed that time had stopped and the indescribable roaring of the earth would never end. Dr Iannis rushed out of the room that used to be Pelagia's and spoke for the first time in years. 'Get out! Get out!' he cried. 'It's an earthquake! Save yourselves!' His voice sounded small and far away, and immediately afterwards he was thrown violently sideways.

More frightened than they had ever been in their lives, the two women stumbled towards the door, were thrown down and attempted to crawl. But again and again they were thrown upwards and sideways and, unable to crawl on their hands and knees, they spread their hands and legs and moved towards the door like snakes, reaching it just as the roof began to fall in.

Outside in the yard dust was slowly rising as the earth went up and down, while in the centre of the street a stream of water suddenly rose to a height of twelve metres and then disappeared as if it had never been. Houses suddenly leapt upwards and solid stone walls moved like paper in the wind, and then suddenly there was a stillness like that of death.

Pelagia, spitting and covered in dirt, filled with a sense of utter helplessness, began to struggle to her knees. Suddenly the strange silence was broken by the wild cries of the priest, who rushed from the church with his arms raised to heaven. 'You pig!' he roared. 'You evil dog!' He fell to his knees and, with tears in his eyes, struck at the earth with his fists.

At this point, as if in response to his cries, the terrible roaring began again and once more the Cephallonian earth danced, the peaks of the mountains rocking like boats. During those intervals when the motion stopped, Pelagia, Drosoula and Antonia held tightly on to each other, gazing in horror at the old house, of which there was little left. The walls were reduced to half their height and the roof lay in ruins on the floor. This ruin contained the sad soul and tired old body of the doctor, who had planned his last words for years and now died beneath the stones without the chance to say them.

◆

The British were the first to arrive, sending four large ships carrying water, food, medicines, doctors and rescue equipment. Italy, remembering its shameful past, sent ships loaded with rescue workers, and American ships arrived carrying earthmovers, helicopters and 3,000 sailors. The Greek Navy turned up late but eager, and the King of Greece and his family travelled around the islands. The earthmovers began the slow work of clearing the ruined houses, and foreign aid workers built cities of tents as temporary accommodation for the islanders. Aeroplanes and helicopters dropped food to hillside communities whose roads had been cut off by the earthquake.

In Cephallonia, because of the wide streets and the fact that most buildings were only one storey high, few people actually died in the earthquake. There were the usual stories concerning people who had lost their sense of time and appeared from beneath the ruins of houses after nine days, believing it had been a few hours.

The islanders reacted differently, according to whether or not they found a natural leader among themselves. Where none appeared, people became sad and purposeless and had terrible dreams of falling into endless space. During the earthquake itself perhaps a quarter of the islanders, like the doctor, had remained calm, but afterwards the remaining three-quarters suffered terrible shame remembering the way they had abandoned their children and elderly parents.

Although he had always been considered a slow-thinking man, Velisarios, who was now forty-two years old and stronger than he had ever been, took command in Pelagia's village. With a strength that seemed greater than that of the earthquake itself, he threw off the beams and stones that imprisoned the crushed body of the doctor, because he was aware that decay was followed by disease. Then he gathered together the confused and hopeless villagers and ordered them into small working parties.

For months after the earthquake, there were times when the earth would shake and tremble, not violently as it had done in the earthquake itself, but enough to make people scream in fear. It was Velisarios who told people to get back to work, threatening them with broken bones unless they returned to their tasks. Even Pelagia, who was almost crazy with grief, was given the work of caring for people's wounds, while Drosoula, who at first could only cry, was put in charge of the children so that their parents could work.

When the aid workers finally arrived at the village, they found a small community living in tents made of sheets of iron, with toilets dug at a safe distance from the water supply. An enormous man was in charge, who in old age would be more loved and respected than the teacher or the priest.

For three months the earth moved, as if it was breathing. Then, at last, it became quiet and motionless once again, and reconstruction began, to be completed three years later. Ancient and beautiful Italian towns were rebuilt as plain white boxes. Pelagia's village was put up further down the hill and her old house was abandoned, the contents of the hiding-hole in the kitchen buried, it seemed, forever.

◆

The earthquake changed lives so greatly that, even today, it is still the most important topic of conversation in Cephallonia.

Islanders cannot resist informing strangers of the facts, and tourist guides will mention the earthquake when it seemed they were only going to discuss the weather. Old people remember an event according to whether it was before or after the earthquake. The disaster caused people to recall the war as unimportant by comparison, and they woke up each morning amazed and grateful to be alive.

In the new house that Pelagia, Drosoula and Antonia now lived in, Pelagia's guilt was the central issue in the three women's lives; the thought that she had played a part in her father's death made Pelagia suffer horribly.

'He was seventy,' said Drosoula sensibly. 'It was better to die quickly like that, trying to save us.'

But Pelagia could not accept this. She knew that in the moment of disaster, her mind had been spinning with nothing except the need to save herself, and she knew that when her father had fallen she should have tried, even at the risk of her own life, to drag him through the door before the roof fell in. She fell into a bottomless pit of self-blame, took no interest in her appearance and did not perform her household tasks, preferring to sit by the doctor's grave, chewing her lips until they bled. With her untidy greying hair and her pale face, she simply sat and watched, as if expecting his ghost to rise up through the earth and speak to her. Time after time, in the winter storms and rains, Drosoula and Antonia would go to the grave and drag Pelagia away, while she sighed and wept.

One day Antonia and Drosoula could stand no more; they began to feel impatient and angry, and the old woman and the young girl discussed how they could cure Pelagia of her sorrow.

'Why don't we just tie her to the bed and hit her?' suggested Antonia.

Drosoula sighed with pleasure at the thought and for a moment wondered whether or not it would work. Then her eyes brightened and she kissed the young girl on the top of her forehead. 'I've had an idea,' she said.

At breakfast the next morning, Antonia suddenly announced, 'I had a dream about Granddad last night.'

'That's funny,' said Drosoula, 'so did I.'

They looked at Pelagia for some kind of reaction, but she simply continued to tear a piece of bread into tiny pieces.

'He told me he was glad he was dead,' said Antonia, 'because now he can be with Mama's mother.'

'That's not what he told me,' replied Drosoula, and Pelagia asked, 'Why are you talking as if I'm not here?'

'Because you're not,' replied Drosoula truthfully. 'You haven't been here for a long time.'

'What did he tell you then?' enquired Antonia.

'He told me that he wants Mama to write the History of Cephallonia that got buried in the earthquake. He said it spoils the fun of being dead, knowing that it's got lost.'

Pelagia regarded them suspiciously and Antonia asked her innocently, 'So are you going to write it?'

'There's no point in asking her,' said Drosoula. 'She's on another planet.'

'That's not true,' protested Pelagia.

'Welcome back,' said Drosoula rudely.

Pelagia went back to her father's grave and thought about what Drosoula had said; although she knew that the story of the dream was nonsense, it occurred to her that rewriting the History would indeed be a way to keep her father's spirit alive. She travelled into Argostoli and returned with pens and a thick pad of paper.

It was surprisingly easy. Although the History had been destroyed in the earthquake, she had read it so many times that the old phrases rolled through the kitchen door and flowed down her arm and right hand into her pen:

'The ancient, half-forgotten island of Cephallonia rises from the Ionian Sea . . .'

Drosoula and Antonia spied on her as she sat at her table, tapping her teeth with her pen. They crept away to a safe distance, embraced each other and danced.

Pelagia almost became the doctor. She did hardly any housework, leaving it all to the women. Her father's pipe had been found in the ruins of the old house, and she stuck it between her teeth as he had done, but did not light it. She began to add small details to the text that she remembered so well, supplying information about such matters as clothes and baking, and the cruel but traditional treatment of widows. The joy of the work caused a deep change in her. She sent letters of enquiry to universities and discovered that all over the world there were people who loved knowledge so much that they would spend months making enquiries on her behalf.

Finally, at the end of 1961, she put her completed work into an enormous file and wondered what to do next. She learnt from publishers that such a book would have no market and was advised instead to give it to a university. 'I will when I'm dead,' thought Pelagia, and she left it proudly on her shelf as visible evidence of the fact that she was an intellectual in the tradition of the Ancient Greeks.

By this time Antonia was a fresh and beautiful seventeen-year-old, who opposed her adopted mother's ideas as a matter of principle, and the two would sit up late into the night discussing philosophy. 'When you're my age, you'll look back and see I was right,' Pelagia would say.

Antonia had no intention of reaching Pelagia's age and said so. 'I want to die before I'm twenty-five,' she said. 'I don't want to get old. You old people caused all the problems and it's us young ones who have to solve them.'

'Enjoy your dreams,' commented Pelagia.


## Chapter 15    Alexi

It was about this time that mysterious postcards in rather poor Greek began to arrive from all over the world. From Santa Fe came one that said, 'You would like it here. All the houses are made of mud.' From London: 'Mad people: terrible fog.' From Madrid: 'Too hot. Everyone asleep.'

Although Pelagia's first thought was that her father's ghost was visiting his favourite countries and was sending her communications from beyond the grave, her second thought was that they might be from Antonio. But he too was dead. Perhaps, she thought, these unsigned cards were from someone with whom she had exchanged letters during the writing of the History. Puzzled but pleased, she tied her collections of cards together and put them in a box.

'You've got a secret boyfriend,' suggested Antonia, who was pleased to discuss the matter since it drew attention away from her own romantic affairs, which both Pelagia and Drosoula were attempting to discourage.

They had met while Antonia was earning a little money by serving coffee in a café on the *plaza** of Argostoli. There had been a noisy band playing in the square, and the gentleman who had had to rise and shout his order in the young girl's ear had at the same moment realized what a deliciously attractive ear it was. Antonia had also realized that here was a man whose eyes expressed exactly the correct mixture of strength and gentleness, calmness and humour.

Alexi waited at the café day after day, choosing the same table whenever he could, his heart bursting with his desire to see the tall young woman with her perfect teeth and long fingers. She brought him his coffee eagerly, forbidding the other girls, the waiters, and even the owner himself to serve him. One day he took her hand while she was putting down a cup, looked passionately up at her and said, 'Marry me.'

Alexi was a lawyer whose skilful speeches could make a judge weep, but while Pelagia recognized his excellence in this area, she could not stand the thought of him marrying Antonia. She was very tall, he was short. She was only seventeen, and he was

* *plaza*: Greek for *square*.

thirty-two. She was tall and graceful, he was overweight and had a habit of tripping over things. Pelagia remembered her passion for Mandras at the same age and forbade the marriage, certain that this was the right thing to do.

The wedding day was nevertheless delightful. Antonia, beaming with happiness, kissed even the strangers who had come to stare, and Alexi, sweating with alcohol and joy, made a long and extremely poetic speech, much of it very wisely in praise of his mother-in-law. She would always remember the exact moment during the celebrations when she had seen what it was about him that had awakened Antonia's heart. It was when he put his arm around her, kissed her on the cheek and said, 'We are going to buy a house in your village, with your permission.' The humble tone of his voice and his implied doubt that she might not want him near her was enough to cause her to become extremely fond of him.

While Pelagia waited impatiently for a grandchild, Drosoula became deeply involved in work. In the empty space by the harbour that had once been her own house, she put up a wooden roof and some romantic lamps. She borrowed some ancient tables and chairs, bought a cheap oven and grandly started the *taverna*★ that she would run eccentrically but with great success until the day of her death in 1972.

It was the 1960s, and tourists were just beginning to arrive in Cephallonia. Wealthy boat owners passed on information to their friends about the most unusual places to eat. German soldiers who had turned into gentle citizens with vast families brought their sons and daughters and told them, 'This is where Daddy was in the war. Isn't it beautiful?' Italians arrived by ferry, bringing their pretty white dogs. Consequently, as the owner of the only *taverna* in the little port, Drosoula earned enough in the summer to do nothing at all in the winter.

★ *taverna*: a small, inexpensive restaurant.

Lemoni, who was now married, immensely fat and the mother of three children, helped with the serving, and Pelagia came down, taking the opportunity to practise her Italian. The service was not fast; to tell the truth, it was extremely slow. The guests were treated unapologetically as members of Drosoula's patient family, and quite often there was no service at all if Drosoula happened to like a particular customer with whom she was deep in conversation. The foreigners, who loved and feared her, never complained about her forgetfulness and her indefinite delays, and would say, 'She's so nice, poor old thing, it seems a shame to hurry her.'

Meanwhile, year after year, Pelagia waited for a grandchild that never came. 'It's my body,' declared Antonia, 'and I have the right to choose. Anyway, the world's population is already too large. Alexi agrees with me, so don't think you can go and shout at him.'

'I'm getting old,' Pelagia would say, 'that's all.'

Time passed. It was Drosoula who died first, perfectly upright in her rocking chair, so quietly that it seemed she was apologizing for having lived at all. She was a courageous woman who had lived a few short years of happiness with a husband that she had loved, a woman who had rejected her son as a matter of principle and lived the rest of her days in willing service to her adopted family.

After Drosoula was buried near the doctor, Pegalia realized that she was now truly alone. She had no idea any more how to run a life, and it was with fear and hopelessness in her heart that she took over Drosoula's *taverna* and attempted to make a living.

Alexi, who by his early thirties had lost all his hair, achieved success as a lawyer, as Pelagia had known he would, and acquired, among other things, a big Citroen car. When at last, in 1979, Antonia gave in to the demands of nature and became pregnant, she and Alexi started to hold hands again in public, stared dreamily at babies and made long lists of possible names.

'It's going to be a girl,' said Pelagia. 'Really, you must call her Drosoula.'

'But Drosoula was so big and . . .'

'Ugly? It doesn't matter. We loved her anyway. Her name should live.'

'Oh, I don't know, Mama . . .'

'I am an old woman,' declared Pelagia, who gained great satisfaction from repeating this statement. 'It might be my last wish.'

'You're sixty. These days that isn't old.'

'Well, I feel old.'

'You don't look it.'

'I didn't bring you up to be a liar,' said Pelagia, terribly pleased, nevertheless.

'I'm thirty-four,' said Antonia. 'That's old.'

When the little boy appeared, Pelagia began to refer to the child as Iannis, and she did this so frequently that it soon seemed obvious to its parents that it could not be called by any other name. If you called it Iannis, it smiled and blew bubbles, so Iannis it was.

Alexi, now realizing that a man must pass something on to his son, began to look around for good investments. He built a small block of holiday apartments and installed a modern kitchen and toilets in the *taverna*. He persuaded Pelagia to allow him to hire a proper cook, leaving her as the manager, and they split the profits fifty-fifty. On the white walls Pelagia stuck all the postcards that continued to arrive from the four corners of the world.


## Chapter 16   An Unexpected Lesson

At five years old, Iannis, who spent nearly all his time at the *taverna* in his grandmother's care, already knew how to say 'Hello' and 'Isn't he sweet?' in six different languages. The reason for his continual presence at the 'Taverna Drosoula' was that his father was building new holiday apartments and tennis courts and his mother was opening shops that sold cheap souvenirs all over the island. Their son grew up contentedly in his grandmother's company, playing in the clear waters of the port and slowly learning the Italian that Pelagia insisted on speaking to him. In the evening, the reunited family would sit together in the *taverna*, arguing both in Italian and in Greek, while Pelagia would embarrass Iannis with references to his infant years.

When he was ten years old, Pelagia hired a *bozouki*★ player to entertain her guests in the *taverna*. His name was Spiridon and he played his *bozouki* with such skill that he could persuade even the Germans to put their arms around each other's shoulders and dance in a circle while stamping on the floor. Iannis loved Spiridon, with his broad shoulders and his wide mouth that seemed to contain a hundred flashing teeth. Pelagia also loved him because he reminded her of her long-lost captain, and occasionally her heart wished desperately for a time-machine to take her back to the days of the only real love of her life.

Iannis did not fail to notice that Spiridon was popular with women, who at the end of every performance would seize the red roses from the vases in the middle of their tables, and throw them at him. So one day Iannis demanded that Spiridon should teach him how to play the *bozouki*.

'Your arms aren't long enough yet,' said Spiro. 'It would make more sense to start with a mandolin. It's the same thing really, but small enough for you.'

'Will you teach me to play it?'

'Of course, but we'll have to find a mandolin. Otherwise we might have to do just the theory.'

★ *bozouki*: a long-necked, stringed Greek musical instrument, related to the mandolin.

Iannis begged his mother and father to get him one, and they promised to buy one when they next went to Athens, but forgot. Eventually Pelagia told him, 'In fact we have one already, but it's buried under the old house. I am sure Antonio wouldn't mind you digging it up.'

'Who's Antonio?'

'My Italian fiancé who was killed in the war. It belonged to him. There was a big trapdoor in the middle of the floor and it was in a hole underneath.'

So Iannis dragged Spiridon up the hill and showed him a ghostly ruin overgrown with long grass, its broken stones just visible above the growth. All around it lay the silent and deserted remains of lonely little houses.

'It's the saddest place,' said Iannis. 'I come here to explore sometimes.' He pointed. 'My grandfather died in there. I'm named after him. Grandma says he was the best doctor in Greece and that he could cure people by touching them.'

The two of them went through what had once been the door and scratched their heads when they saw the rubbish that lay all around. Spiro blew out his cheeks and sighed. 'We've got two days work here,' he said. 'We'll just have to get on with it.'

By the next evening there was a clear space in the middle of the old floor and the trapdoor lay revealed in the area that had once been the kitchen. Spiro tried to get his fingers under the iron ring of the door but, hard as he tried, he could not move it. He and the child were gazing at the ring and scratching their heads when they became aware of a very big old man in a black suit, standing a little bent in the doorway. 'What are you doing?' he asked. 'Oh, it's you, young Iannis. I thought you were looters.'

'We're trying to open this,' said the boy. 'It's stuck, and it's got something inside that we want.'

The old man came inside and examined the trapdoor with his watery eyes before slowly bending down and putting the tips of

93

the fingers of one hand under the iron ring. He leaned sideways, putting all his weight and strength into lifting the ring and, with a sudden loud crack, the door flew upwards in a cloud of dust. Velisarios rubbed his hands together, blew on the tips of his fingers and seemed suddenly to become a tired old man again. 'Goodbye, my friends,' he said, and made his way slowly down the path to the new village.

'Unbelievable,' said Spiro.

Inside the hiding-place, in perfect condition, they found an antique German record player, a handmade blanket, a bundle of papers written in Italian and another package of papers with the title, 'A Personal History of Cephallonia'. There was also a cloth bundle containing the most beautiful mandolin that Spiro had ever seen.

When Iannis showed Pelagia the mandolin, she started crying and, to Iannis's amazement, she did not stop for a whole week. Iannis comforted her as best he could, climbing on to her knees, which he was really a little too old for, and wiping her tears, wondering how it was possible to love an old woman with stiff knees and thin grey hair so much. While Iannis comforted Pelagia, Spiro carefully cleaned and polished the mandolin. He tightened and tuned each string and told Iannis, with great seriousness, that the mandolin was the most precious thing he would ever own, so that Iannis learned to regard the instrument with a respect that he had never felt in church, when dragged there by Pelagia.

◆

In October 1993 Iannis was fourteen, and he had had a whole summer in which to play in public with Spiridon and have red roses thrown at him. In order not to annoy his grandmother with his constant practising – in fact not to make her cry again – he had gone up to the ruins of the old house to play in private, and was concentrating very hard on a particularly difficult piece of music. He was biting his lip with the effort, and did not notice an old man who approached him and watched him with critical but delighted interest. Iannis nearly jumped out of his seat when a voice said, in a very strange accent, 'Excuse me, young man.'

'Ah!' Iannis exclaimed. 'You frightened me.'

'I couldn't help noticing,' said the man, 'that you are doing something wrong.'

'I know, I'm having trouble with this piece,' replied Iannis, noticing how unusually bright-eyed the old man was, and how there was about him an atmosphere of energy and laughter.

'Let me show you how to place your fingers.' The old man came over to Iannis and started to pull the boy's fingers into place, explaining as he did so why the fingers were better in this position. Then he stood upright and added, 'You can always tell a really good musician because a good musician doesn't seem to be moving his fingers at all.'

'You seem to know a lot about it,' said Iannis.

'Well, I ought to. I've been a professional mandolin player for nearly all my life. I can tell that you're going to be good.'

'Play me something?' asked the boy, offering him the mandolin. The old man took the mandolin, settled it into this body and began to play in such a way that Iannis's mouth fell open with amazement. Suddenly the old man stopped, turned the mandolin over, examined it with an expression of disbelief and exclaimed, 'Mother of God, it's Antonia.'

'How did you know it's called Antonia?' asked Iannis, both surprised and suspicious. 'Have you seen it before?'

'Where did you find it? Who gave it to you?'

'I dug it out of that hole,' said Iannis, pointing to the open trapdoor. 'Grandma told me it was there.'

'And would your grandmother be *Kyria* Pelagia, daughter of Dr Iannis?'

'That's me. I'm called Iannis, after him.'

The old man sat next to the boy on the wall, still holding the mandolin, and wiped his forehead with a handkerchief, seeming suddenly very anxious. 'Tell me, young man, is your grandmother alive? Is she happy?' he asked finally.

'She cries sometimes, ever since we dug Antonia and all the other things out of the hole.'

'And what about your grandfather? Is he well?'

The boy seemed confused. 'What grandfather?' he asked.

'Not your father's father. I mean *Kyria* Pelagia's husband,' said the old man, wiping his forehead again.

'There isn't one. I didn't even know she had one.'

'Are you saying that *Kyria* Pelagia hasn't got a husband? You haven't got a grandfather?'

'I suppose I must have, but I've never heard of him. I've only got my father's father, and he's half-dead.'

The old man stood up, looked around him and said, 'This was a beautiful place. I had the best years of my life here. And do you know what? I was going to marry your grandmother once. I think it's time I saw her again.'

The two of them were walking down the hill when Iannis stopped suddenly. 'If you're the one who played the mandolin and was going to marry Grandma ... does that mean you're the ghost?' The autumnal sun shone briefly through the cloud, and the old man paused for thought.

## Chapter 17   The Return

Antonio Corelli, although in his seventies, rediscovered a certain youthful energy in his old limbs as he danced about, trying to avoid being hit by the frying pans that Pelagia was busily throwing at him. 'You pig!' she screamed. 'All my life waiting, all my life thinking you were dead. And you alive and me a fool. How can you break such promises? Betrayer!'

Corelli backed against the wall, trying to hold off the broomstick that Pelagia was waving at him. 'I told you,' he cried. 'I thought you were married.'

'Married!' she exclaimed bitterly. 'No such luck! Thanks to you, you rat.' She made a move as if she was going to hit him across the head with the broom handle.

'I came back for you. 1946. I came round the bend and there you were with the little baby, looking so happy.'

'Was I married? Who told you that? So I adopt a baby that someone leaves on my doorstep . . . Couldn't you have said, "Excuse me, but is this your baby?"'

'Please stop hitting me. I came back every year, you know I did. You saw me, I always saw you with the child. I was so bitter I couldn't speak. But I had to see you.'

'Bitter? I don't believe my ears. You? Bitter?'

'For ten years,' said Corelli, 'for ten years I was so bitter that I even wanted to kill you. And then I thought, well, OK, I was away for three years, perhaps she thought I wasn't coming back, perhaps she thought I was dead, perhaps she thought I'd forgotten, perhaps she met someone else and fell in love. As long as she's happy. But I still came back, every year, just to see you were all right. Is that betrayal?'

'And did you ever see a husband? And did you think what it did to me when I ran to you and you disappeared? Did you think about my heart?'

'OK, so I jumped the wall and hid. I had to. I thought you were married, I told you. Pelagia, please, this is a terrible embarrassment for the customers. Can't we go for a walk and talk about it on the beach?'

She looked round at all the faces, some of them grinning, some of them pretending to look the other way. Everywhere there were overturned chairs and tables that Pelagia had thrown to the floor in her anger. 'You should have died,' she shouted, 'and left me with my dreams. You never loved me.' She marched out of the door, leaving Corelli bowing repeatedly to the customers and saying, 'Please excuse us.'

Two hours later they were sitting on a familiar rock, gazing out over the sea at the yellow lights of the harbour reflected in the blackened waters. 'I see you got my postcards, then,' he said.

'In Greek. Why did you learn Greek?'

'I was ashamed of being an invader. I was so ashamed that I didn't want to be Italian any more. I've been living in Athens for about twenty-five years. I'm a Greek citizen.'

'Did you become a composer?'

'Yes, I've played my music all over the world. I wrote my first big piece of music for you. It's called "Pelagia's March".' He noticed that she was trying not to cry, and thought how emotional she had become in her old age. She had even knocked out his false teeth, so that they had fallen in the sand and had to be washed in the sea.

'I feel like an unfinished poem,' said Pelagia, with a heavy sigh. Corelli felt a sting of shame and avoided a reply.

'Everything's changed. Everything here used to be so pretty and now the houses look like boxes made of cement.'

'And we have electricity and telephones and running water and proper toilets and earthquake-resistant houses. Is that so bad?'

There was a silence, during which the thoughts of both of them returned to the past. 'I see you still have my ring,' he said.

'Only because I couldn't get it off,' she answered. 'I had it altered to fit and now I regret it.' She hesitated. 'So did you get married? I suppose you did.'

'Me? No. As I said, I was very bitter for years and years. I was horrible to everyone, especially women, and then I became successful and I was all over the world, flying from one place to another. And, anyway, who wants to be with someone who is dreaming of someone else?'

'Antonio Corelli, I can see that you can still tell lies with your silver tongue. And how can you bear to look at me now? I'm an old woman. I feel ashamed to be so old and ugly. You look the same, just old and thin, but I look like someone else, I know it. I want you to remember me properly. Now I'm just a lump.'

'You forget that I came to spy on you. If you see things happen gradually, there's no shock. You're just the same.' He squeezed her hand gently and said, 'Don't worry, it's still Pelagia. Pelagia with a bad temper, but still Pelagia.'

'Did you ever think that I might have been raped and that was why I had a baby?'

'Yes, I did.'

'And . . . ?'

'I admit it made a difference. We had some ideas about dishonour then, didn't we? Thank God we're not so stupid now.'

'The man who tried to rape me . . . I shot him.'

He looked at her in disbelief. 'You shot him?'

'I was never dishonoured. He was the fiancé I had before you.'

'You never said anything about a fiancé.'

'Jealous?'

'Of course I'm jealous.' The emotion was beginning to stir him a little too much and he tried to control his feelings. Pelagia decided it was time to change the subject. 'I want to show you something. You never read Carlo's papers, did you? Come back to the *taverna* and eat, and I'll give you his writing. We do an excellent snails dish.'

'Snails!' he exclaimed. 'I remember all about snails.'

Corelli sat at the table with its plastic cloth and read through the stiff old sheets that had curled up at the corners. As he read, he frowned, and once or twice he blinked as if in disbelief. When

99

he had finished reading, Pelagia came and sat opposite him. 'Well?' she asked.

He tapped the pile of papers. 'I wish you hadn't shown me these. I'm more old-fashioned than I thought. I had no idea.'

'He loved you. Are you disgusted?'

'Sad . . . It's a shock. I can't help it.'

'He wasn't just another hero, was he? He was more complicated. Poor Carlo.'

They began to talk more freely. 'Are you very famous then?' Pelagia asked.

'Only in the sense that other musicians have heard of me. I've retired now . . . In fact, I was thinking . . . I want to rebuild the old house. I want to live in a nice place. A place with memories.'

'Without water and electricity?'

'I'll put them in. Would you sell me the site?'

'You're insane. I don't even know if we own it.'

'Then you don't mind. I'd pay you to come and clean it,' he said wickedly.

She took him seriously. 'What? Do I need money? With this *taverna*? Go home to Athens. Anyway, Lemoni would do it.'

'Little Lemoni? She's still here?'

'She's as big as a ship and a grandmother.'

He fell silent again, remembering the past, then said, 'So do I have your permission to rebuild the house?'

'No,' she said, still holding on to her anger.

'Oh.' He looked at her doubtfully. He would return to the topic at a later date, he decided. 'I'm going to come and see you tomorrow,' he said, 'with a surprise.'

'I don't want any surprises. Go to hell with your surprises. You owe me a life.'

'Ah. I'll bring you a life then.'

'Stupid old man.'

He turned up the next day with screaming brakes in a cloud

of blue smoke. Pelagia shook her head disapprovingly as he climbed carefully off the motorbike, which was bright red and looked as if it had been designed for racing. 'Do you know where we're going?' the captain said. 'We're going to see if Casa Nostra is still there . . .' he tapped the machine '. . . on a motorbike.'

'Do you really think the hut survived the earthquake? And do you really think I'm going on a thing like that? At my age?'

'I hired it specially. It goes very well.'

'No,' she said. 'My knees are too stiff.'

'Don't you want to see Casa Nostra?'

'Not with a madman.'

'I've got it for two days. We can sit on a rock and watch the sea.'

It took a long time to persuade her. As they swung dangerously from side to side along the stony roads, she held on tightly to his waist, her face buried between his shoulders. Corelli noticed that she held on to him even more desperately than in the old days, and from time to time he deliberately swung to one side of the road so that she would hold him tighter. 'May the saints save me,' thought Pelagia, and in search of safety slid her arms right round his waist and linked her fingers together.

# ACTIVITIES

## Chapters 1–3

*Before you read*

1 A large part of *Captain Corelli's Mandolin* takes place during the Second World War. Discuss these questions about the war.
   a When did it begin and end?
   b Which were the main countries on each side?
   c Who were their leaders?
   d Which country began the war?
   e Which countries won?

2 Find the words in *italics* in your dictionary. They are all used in the story. Discuss possible connections between these pairs.
   a *broom    sigh*
   b *conquest    oppress*
   c *gaze    passion*
   d *invade    rape*

3 Match these words with a definition below.
   *cannon    exclaim    feast    flirt    homosexual*
   a A person who is sexually attracted to people of the same sex
   b An old type of heavy gun that fired metal balls
   c A religious festival
   d To speak loudly and suddenly
   e To behave in a romantic way without serious intentions

*After you read*

4 What do you know about each of these people or places?
   a Cephallonia          d Mandras
   b Dr Iannis            e Velisarios
   c Pelagia              f Carlo

5 In these three chapters there are examples of comedy and of tragedy. Discuss some examples of each, and which section you enjoyed most and why.

## Chapters 4–7

*Before you read*

6  Do you think that Pelagia and Mandras are suited to each other? Do you think that they will actually get married? Give reasons for your opinion.

7  Find these words in your dictionary.

*blink   compose   embrace   stumble   weep*

Which of these actions do you do with your:

a  eyes?      b  legs?      c  arms?      d  brain?

8  Answer these questions. Find the words in *italics* in your dictionary.

a  What are you planning to do if you have a *fiancé* or a *fiancée*?

b  Do people sing or play a *mandolin*?

c  Do you find a *trapdoor* in a floor or a garden?

d  What do *troops* do?

*After you read*

9  Answer these questions.

a  Why does Pelagia get depressed?

b  Why is Pelagia so shocked by Mandras's return?

c  Why does the doctor hide his 'History of Cephallonia'?

d  Why does Captain Corelli come to stay at the doctor's house?

e  Why are Velisarios and Carlo friendly towards each other?

10  Terrible changes happen to Mandras. What are they? Do you think they are understandable? Give reasons for your opinion.

11  Describe Captain Corelli from the point of view of:

a  Pelagia              b  Dr Iannis              c  Carlo

12  How do Pelagia's feelings about Captain Corelli change as the story progresses?

## Chapters 8–10

*Before you read*

13  Discuss these questions. What do you think?

a  How will Mandras re-enter the story?

**b** How will the relationship between Pelagia and the captain progress?

14 Answer the questions. Find the words in *italics* in your dictionary.

    **a** Where might you find each of these things?

      *briars  goggles  loot  snail  undergrowth*

    **b** What does the word *arms* mean in this sentence?

      The soldiers put down their arms and surrendered.

*After you read*

15 Explain the part that the following play in the story:

    snails  a motorbike  Casa Nostra  Bunnios  La Scala

16 General Gandin makes a terrible mistake. What is the mistake? Why does he make it? What is the tragic result?

17 Do you agree that Carlo is a hero? Give reasons for your opinion.

**Chapters 11–13**

*Before you read*

18 What do you think will happen to Captain Corelli now?

19 Find these words in your dictionary. Use both words in a sentence.

    *inject  morphia*

*After you read*

20 Who says these things? To whom? Explain the situation.

    **a** 'I have no equipment to perform an operation.'

    **b** 'I swear by all the saints that this man's flesh is made of steel.'

    **c** 'If I am caught, I should die alone.'

    **d** 'This is an Italian soldier and we have to get him out.'

    **e** 'Go well, Antonio, and return.'

21 Explain how, in Chapter 12, life becomes tragic for Pelagia, Dr Iannis and the islanders. Explain how, in contrast, events happen in Chapter 13 that comfort Pelagia.

**22** Work with a partner. Act out the conversation that Pelagia has with Drosoula after she sees Corelli's ghost.

## Chapters 14–17

*Before you read*

**23** What is your reaction to the appearance of Captain Corelli's ghost? How do you think the novel will end?

*After you read*

**24** Complete these sentences.

    **a** Dr Iannis saves Pelagia and Drosoula's lives by ...

    **b** Velisarios helps the villagers by ...

    **c** In the end, Pelagia recovers from her guilt and grief for her father by ...

    **d** At first, Pelagia does not think Alexi is suitable for Antonia because ...

    **e** Pelagia becomes fond of Alexi when she realizes that ...

    **f** Drosoula makes money by ...

    **g** Pelagia's life becomes much happier because ...

    **h** Iannis wants to play the *bozouki* because ...

    **i** Velisarios helps Iannis by ...

    **j** Corelli is astonished when Iannis tells him that ...

**25** Explain how Corelli has spent the last fifty years since he left Pelagia, and why he did not return to her. Do you find his explanation realistic? Why (not)?

## Writing

**26** Write a letter that Pelagia might have written to Mandras after he leaves Cephallonia to join the army.

**27** Describe the changes in Pelagia's life, and how Pelagia changes as she experiences them.

**28** In your opinion, who is the finest character in the novel? Give reasons for your opinion.

29 'In *Captain Corelli's Mandolin*, the author explores different kinds of love.' Discuss this statement.

30 Why do you think the novel is called *Captain Corelli's Mandolin*? What does the mandolin represent, do you think?

31 Imagine that after the killing of the Italians, Weber writes a document explaining his part in it. Write that document.

LR

Answers for the Activities in this book are published in our free resource packs for teachers, the Penguin Readers Factsheets, or available on a separate sheet. Please write to your local Pearson Education office or to: Marketing Department, Penguin Longman Publishing, 5 Bentinck Street, London W1M 5RN.